Draco felt a surge of contempt remembering the days after she had humiliated him, how he had lain awake at night aching for her.

Now he looked at her and admired the tilt of her nose, the wide-spaced dramatically green eyes, the kissable lips and the stubborn tilt of her chin...

"Were you looking for me?" Jane asked.

He straightened up and looked down at her. "Was I meant to look for you?"

Had she anticipated he would? Had she expected that reaction? Had she engineered this situation? He had not chased after his fleeing bride. To do so would have made him his father—a man who had been so obsessed with a woman that it had broken him.

If he'd believed in fate, he would have said it was meant to be, but Draco believed that a man made his own fate.

"No, I didn't expect that," she said quietly, adding huskily, "Why are you here?"

With his mouth lifted into a lazy self-mocking half smile, he asked himself the same question now.

Was this an opportunity? If so, for what? Revenge?

Kim Lawrence lives on a farm in Anglesey with her university-lecturer husband, assorted pets who arrived as strays and never left, and sometimes one or both of her boomerang sons. When she's not writing, she loves to be outdoors gardening or walking on one of the beaches for which the island is famous—along with being the place where Prince William and Catherine made their first home!

Books by Kim Lawrence

Harlequin Presents

Claimed by Her Greek Boss
Awakened in Her Enemy's Palazzo

A Ring from a Billionaire

Waking Up in His Royal Bed
The Italian's Bride on Paper

Jet-Set Billionaires

Innocent in the Sicilian's Palazzo

The Secret Twin Sisters

The Prince's Forbidden Cinderella
Her Forbidden Awakening in Greece

Visit the Author Profile page
at Harlequin.com for more titles.

HIS WEDDING DAY REVENGE

KIM LAWRENCE

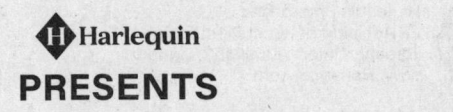

PRESENTS

H Harlequin®
PRESENTS™

ISBN-13: 978-1-335-93928-9

His Wedding Day Revenge

Harlequin Enterprises ULC
22 Adelaide St. West, 41st Floor
Toronto, Ontario M5H 4E3, Canada
www.Harlequin.com

Printed in Lithuania

MIX
Paper | Supporting responsible forestry
FSC® C021394

HIS WEDDING DAY
REVENGE

PROLOGUE

FEDERICO ALLOWED HIMSELF a small smile of professional satisfaction as he flicked through the unedited frames he and his team had taken so far.

Obviously he didn't normally do weddings, but this was no ordinary event. The wedding of the decade was not that original, but neither was it an exaggeration considering the guest list and the news and social media coverage today had attracted.

Some cynics had suggested the timing had more to do with practicality than romance as many of the international high-profile guests had not had to travel far. Many had been in the UK for the previous night's awards ceremony for young innovators in environmental sustainability sponsored by the groom, who had spent the last couple of months in London to smooth the transition of his latest UK-based high-tech acquisition.

Cynics aside, the event had captured the public imagination—everyone was talking about it.

Except the happy couple.

Draco Andreas was known to be a man of few words and all of them to the point. Though it was said that being on the receiving end of a glare from him was worth several thousand-page volumes of words!

As for the bride, well... Normally people speculated about the dress, but in this case the speculation was about the bride herself. There were only a couple of grainy out-of-focus snapshots circulating online of the prospective Mrs Andreas, which showed she was a redhead, or had been when they were taken, and she was petite.

The mystery had upped the feverish interest in the woman who had bagged the man whose name had become a global brand in the space of eight years. Conspiracy theories abounded on the Internet from the crazy to the crazier.

Federico was just as curious as everyone else and he didn't have long to wait now, according to the schedule he'd been given. He glanced at his watch: two minutes.

He had no doubt that it would be two minutes. The entire event had been organised with nothing short of military precision. Nothing had been left to chance. Even the weather had defied the forecast, which he was happy about. He might be a genius but there was no harm having the weather on his side.

All he had to do now was make the bride look good. He assumed this would not be difficult as he'd never seen a woman who was less than knockout gorgeous on the arm of Draco Andreas, though up until now none had stayed attached very long!

There were jealous individuals who suggested that wealth was a well-known aphrodisiac but, if half the kiss-and-tell tabloid stories were true, even before Draco had been catapulted from relative anonymity to global fame and fortune he'd not exactly had trouble getting a date!

Given his profile today, it was hard to believe that only eight years ago Draco Andreas had inherited the ancestral name and the looks but no money. Most people had expected him to take the route of many land rich but impoverished old families in Italy and elsewhere and sell up, but Andreas had proved to be a man who didn't take the obvious path, and where there wasn't one he built his own.

And he built big!

The mobile app that had been the first thing produced by his tech start-up had revolutionised personal finances for millions globally. Draco was widely held to have been instrumental in changing the financial scene, fostering new technology, supporting innovation and creating a whole new generation of entrepreneurs.

Much of his seemingly limitless energy had gone into his Tuscan family estate, which now showcased creative, forward-thinking green technology, creating jobs and bringing young people back into the depopulated countryside areas.

He did not seek publicity but it sought him. Federico's thoughts turned enviously to the lucky hiker who had captured the recent and already iconic image of the groom-to-be. Draco on horseback complete with sexy stubble, windblown hair and perfect profile looking moody and broody against a magnificent Tuscan sunset as he herded buffalo that apparently supplied the milk for the estate's famous cheese. Well, it was famous now anyway.

Still, you couldn't have everything, including, sadly, an Italian setting, he told himself philosophically. He adjusted a lens and squinted up through the canopy of chestnut trees that lined the driveway to the impressive ancient cathedral that might not have the radiant Tuscan light, but did have its own magical, if austere, aura. His fall-back plan, should the weather break, would not be needed—the sun was shining from a cerulean-blue sky and there was not a cloud in sight.

One of the suited-and-booted security team responded to a voice in his ear and gave the photographer the nod he had been waiting for and he stepped out of the dappled light into the direct sun. He gave a thumbs-up sign to his own team and waited as the crunch of tyres on gravel grew louder.

This was his first sight of the bride, as there had been no informal early glimpses. As accustomed as he was to having the most famous actresses and celebrities pose for him, Federico drew in a sharp breath as she emerged. The bride's days of anonymity were at an end.

His critical professional eye took pleasure in her delicate features, the wide-spaced green eyes and the fact her skin had the pale crystal clarity of the oyster silk gown she wore.

As she completed her graceful exit and stood there, wand slim, the sun catching her burnished hair, he captured the moment. Seriously enjoying himself, he continued to snap. The bride's delicate nose had just the suggestion of a tilt in profile as the solitary bridesmaid bent to straighten her heavy satin train encrusted along the hem with delicate hand-sewn seed pearls.

'Oh, Janie, you look so beautiful, like a dream.'

Jane blinked like someone waking up. Up to this point the entire day had felt like a dream that she had floated through. Floated in the dress that Draco had chosen when she had been unable to make up her mind from all the designer offerings. He'd chosen the flowers too and they were, she decided, making a conscious effort to loosen her death grip on the stems of the hand-tied orchids, beautiful but, sadly, from her point of view, unscented.

She glanced at her small hand as the blood returned to her fingers, the glitter of her ring catching the sun. Draco had said when he slid it on her finger that it matched her eyes, which was why she hadn't liked to say she would have preferred something a little less ostentatious than the heavy square-cut emerald surrounded by diamonds.

It just wasn't her, not as a student holding down three part-time jobs to make ends meet and enjoying the thrill of being in love for the first time... Of having her first lover and her last—which was just as well. Draco would have spoilt her for any other man.

Draco thought the ring was her, and she was trying very hard to be the person he thought she was.

It wasn't just today that felt like a dream. She felt as if she'd been sleepwalking for the past two months, from the first moment she'd seen Draco and their fingers had brushed when she'd dropped to her knees to pick up the by then empty coffee cup she had knocked out of his hands. By the time she'd got to her feet she had been deeply and desperately in lust for the first time in her life.

His first words had been, 'You are perfect.'

Without considering her words, she had blurted with feeling, 'You are beautiful.'

She had spent the night in his hotel bedroom—they had not left it for the next two days and nights.

Having him want her, having him love her—being loved by the most beautiful man she had ever imagined existing—was all a dream, and she didn't want to wake up.

'Are you nervous?'

Was she? Carrie's voice sounded as though it were coming from a long way away.

Jane gave her head a tiny shake. She didn't want to think, she just wanted to be there in the moment. Nothing else mattered but the fact Draco loved her and she loved Draco, she told herself, repeating the words in her head like a mantra to drown out the other voice saying things she didn't want to hear.

'No, I'm not nervous,' she denied, lifting a shaking hand to her mouth, the full contours delicately tinted a pink rose. 'I want this more than anything,' she added with a husky touch of defiance that faded as she confided breathily, 'I just didn't recognise myself when I looked in the mirror. Love, that's what counts, isn't it…?'

Carrie didn't say anything, she just squeezed her friend's cold hand. Jane took a deep breath that lifted her narrow shoulders as she gathered her skirts and took the first step up the flight of shallow stone steps, wondering how many brides had trod this route before her and how many had been happy, how many lived to regret it.

Halfway up, she paused and turned back to her friend.

'Truth matters, doesn't it, Carrie?'

The sudden question made her bridesmaid blink and give a tinkling laugh. 'Don't tell me you have a guilty secret, Janie, because I won't believe you...' Jane gave her a stricken look and the tall brunette's smile faded. 'Last-minute nerves,' she soothed. 'Just take a deep breath.'

Jane nodded and the deep breath took her several steps up the aisle, right up to the moment that Draco, tall and exclusive, her beautiful Italian lover, turned and looked at her. She saw his dark heavy-lidded eyes widen and felt the possessive pulse of heat that radiated from him reach across the space between them.

She wanted to walk, to run into his arms more than anything she had ever wanted, but shame rushed in, cooling the heat inside her and killing all her joy dead.

As their eyes locked she lost her tenuous grip on her denial, along with the flowers, which fell from her fingers, a splash of white on the ancient stone slabs.

Her silence was in itself a lie.

She'd kept the secret to herself for two days.

She'd had two days to tell him, to give him the opportunity to respond, and she hadn't because in her heart she knew what that response would be. Draco wanted a child, an heir for the family acres he spoke of with such passion, and she'd been happy about that because all her life she'd wanted a family, she'd wanted to belong.

After her recent doctor's appointment Jane knew the chances of her giving him that were slim to non-existent.

There would be no baby with Draco's dark hair, she couldn't give him what he wanted and one day he'd know too, and hate her. The ache in her chest became a physical pain that hurt more than the physical pain she'd suffered for so long, a pain that now had a name—endometriosis.

She couldn't do this to him. She loved him too much.

With a small, lost cry, Jane picked up her heavy skirts, tears streaming down her face as she turned and ran.

The silence after the sound of her heels vanished was so deafening it bounced off the ancient rafters. All eyes were on the face of the man standing at the altar, a face that seemed carved from cold stone. The fire was in the flames of icy fury in his eyes.

CHAPTER ONE

THE NARROW COUNTRY lane snaked seemingly endlessly through the English countryside, bordered by unruly hedgerows brightened by hawthorn berries beneath canopies of ancient trees. Another occasion Draco might have enjoyed this corner of rural England he had never visited before.

As he lightly gripped the steering wheel of his sleek black car, the tap of his long, tapering brown fingers was the only outward indicator of the frustration that simmered beneath the surface. The overcast sky loomed, threatening rain that reflected his mood.

He could have done without this! The finger tapping against leather got louder. A visit to the site of a development that had become controversial overnight thanks to an overzealous, impatient site manager out to impress—wow, had that one backfired—was not his idea of a fun trip.

The guy had cut corners that didn't need cutting and outraged vocal locals, who had tapped into several media outlets during a lull in the news cycle and hit a community nerve.

A shiny monster of a tractor lumbered into view,

trundling along at a pace that seemed deliberate in its disregard for Draco's timetable. His annoyance deepened—the driver was acting as though he were invisible.

This wasn't how the CEO of Andreas Company should spend his morning. The corners of his sensually sculpted lips lifted in a half-smile. At least he had not yet lost the ability to laugh at himself...but who would tell him when he did?

The sad truth was, these days, nobody in his life would. It hadn't always been that way, but he hadn't always been a billionaire. People didn't tell billionaires what to do.

A hissing sound of triumph left his clenched teeth as on the fourth attempt he manoeuvred around the tractor and put his foot down.

This controversy could have been avoided—therein lay the core of his frustration. Draco's initial irritation with the situation had now turned to resentment. This was precisely why he had a team—a capable team, at least in theory, which should not necessitate his personal intervention on such a low-level project. But this had gone beyond the project itself or the financial outlay; it was reputational damage that he was here to repair.

The narrow lane suddenly opened up, revealing the expansive stretch of woodland that had stirred the hornets' nest; a few scattered houses and a church spire were visible in the distance.

He saw the site manager just as the guy spotted him and wisely slunk away into the trees. 'Lazy, cost-cutting...' Draco muttered before he slowed and took a deep calming breath. All it needed was a charm offensive and he did not doubt his ability to smooth ruffled feathers and win the locals over.

And it wasn't all PR and damage limitation. Draco believed in this project and he had the facts and figures to back up his belief. The two similar upmarket eco holiday villages in his homeland Italy were up and running, bringing enormous benefits to the local rural communities they were set in.

Recognising early on the scope for financial markets to spur investment in conservation had been partly responsible for his meteoric success. Despite the hype, Draco didn't feel his approach was revolutionary. On the contrary, it was practical and simply about recognising the limits of innovation, engaging with stakeholders and using existing tools.

He scanned the crowd as he drove slowly past, heading to a safe parking spot on the grass ahead, noting the inevitable cameras and microphone-wielding journalists as he searched for someone in the melee who looked to be in charge.

Nobody in the chanting, placard-waving crowd screamed in charge to him, but a guy with a dog collar was holding forth to a news channel; he didn't look too rabid, Draco decided.

He manoeuvred to avoid hitting one of the protesters, who banged his placard on the windscreen, and almost collided with a sign for the Manor Hotel. He caught a glimpse of the building in question through a gap in the trees—a square structure of mellow stone—and wondered about the family who had once lived there.

His own family home in Tuscany could easily have

gone the same way, but, despite the predictions that it
had been inevitable that Draco would have to let it go,
it hadn't and he hadn't.

It never would, not on his watch. He pushed away
the thought. Today wasn't about preserving his family
heritage—that was safe. It was about preserving the
firm's reputation.

Then it happened.

In the periphery of his vision he caught the flash of
vivid red amidst the muted greens and browns of the
countryside. Draco's foot instinctively pressed the brake
pedal, his car slowing to an abrupt halt.

The world seemed to pause, the racket receded, the
air for the space of a breath was sucked out of the car,
leaving a vacuum.

A jolt surged through Draco as recognition, wave
after wave of it, reverberated through his body like an
electric shock.

Jane Smith!

He had never searched for her. He had no interest
in knowing why she had humiliated him, and what her
motivation had been remained a mystery. He had put
thoughts of her, along with the engagement ring that
had landed by courier on his desk, in a deep vault and
thrown away the key, if not literally, certainly mentally
for the past four years.

He had made a conscious decision not to allow her
the courtesy of unpaid space in his head. He had moved
on and he congratulated himself on putting the past behind him.

There had been a few moments of backsliding, but he

did not count the once or twice he had caught sight of a redhead and experienced a gut-clench of anger…mixed with a hunger he would not acknowledge.

On those occasions the blaze of colour in the crowd had turned out to be some generic redhead.

Not this time! There was no double take or 'is it, isn't it?' moment.

Her face was turned away from him, but it didn't matter. It was the way she held herself—almost like a dancer, slender and graceful—the way she tossed her head. The memory of her amazing full-throated laugh escaped the mental box he had walled it up in… He could hear the sound in his head, seeding itself like an old melody you couldn't get out of your mind. A melody that evoked memories, the good among them all cancelled out by that one humiliating final scene, the one that held no laughter. For a split second, that memory was so strong, the moment he had consigned to oblivion was so here, now and in the moment, that he could taste the humiliation in his mouth.

His eyes darkened to midnight, his lack of control over the physical response of his body only adding to the humiliation. That his control, something he took for granted, failed dramatically fed the anger building inside him.

It wasn't the only thing building—the forbidden images stored away for so long were spilling out.

The sun touching her hair and dazzling him.

His skin tingled at the memory of her touch, light like her soft silky hair sweeping his chest as she sat astride him, and her mouth, not light but… Jaw clenched, he pushed back hard at the insidious mesh of intercon-nected images and dragged his focus into the present.

The present where Jane Smith's fiery curls were danc-ing in the wind in stark contrast to the muted tones of the other protesters.

It was only several moments later that he took in the more mundane details: her hair was shorter, more shoulder blade than waist length, and there was…a baby?

The collision of past and present shook loose a raw hoarse sound from his throat. A baby? He felt the mus-cles of his belly tighten in rejection of the image.

Why should she not have a baby? She had moved on, he had moved on… It was simply a twist in the tale that Draco hadn't anticipated.

Anticipated! He mocked himself. As if he had antic-ipated any of this. Why would he? Jane Smith was the past and Draco was a man who lived in the moment.

He could have rejected the flashback but some mas-ochistic part of him allowed it to play out, the moments frozen in time, snapshots of the past, the day they met. Before that day, he would have mocked the idea that the touching of fingers could be erotic.

As he stared at the slim figure, the jeans and boots vanished and she was standing there in a cloud of silk and satin, looking at him with shimmering green eyes and then… The trance broke as Draco distanced him-self ruthlessly from the undertow of emotions—anger, desire. And as he released the foot brake, and the car glided silently forward, tucking into a space, he welcomed the opportunity to prove that Jane Smith meant nothing to him.

Why should he need to prove to himself what he already knew?

Jane stood at the edge of the protest. She was aware that, on her back, Mattie, cocooned in a padded suit, had fallen asleep. His little head complete with bobble hat was pressing against her neck.

He wouldn't be asleep for long. He'd need his next feed and— She stifled a yawn. She could really do with a nap herself. Mattie had been awake most of the night. Sometimes, actually quite often, it seemed to her that he sensed she didn't have a clue what she was doing.

Or maybe he was just angry. She was angry, but Mattie…his loss was incalculable. Onc minute he'd had two beautiful, loving parents and now, because of a stupid accident, he'd got lumbered with her. She glanced around the clearing. Would anyone miss her if she left now?

It wasn't as if the numbers were so few that her absence would be noticed. The cameras, which she had assiduously avoided, had drawn a bigger crowd than expected.

She had turned up at the office of the editor of the local newspaper demanding to be seen, her determination fuelled by righteous indignation and outrage, clutching the proof she'd waved at him, photos of the bulldozers and diggers, the utter devastation, on her phone.

She didn't know what she had expected—an article, a regional radio mention possibly, but definitely not national news. Would she have marched in there if she'd known the name attached to the project that had chopped down the precious trees while the village slept was Andreas?

Jane liked to think she would have.

Andreas... Pathetic really that the name could still evoke such a visceral reaction. It wasn't as if this little project would have registered on Draco's radar. A few trees and up-in-arms locals were definitely below his pay grade!

I really hope it is, she thought. Drawing his attention was the last thing she wanted. She'd moved on.

The sobbing young woman who ran through a church-yard, sidestepped a security guard who looked as if he was about to rugby-tackle her and climbed over a fence, ripping the skirt of her wedding dress to shreds in the process, before she legged it along a cobbled side street—that person seemed like a stranger to her.

She could not imagine what a bedraggled sight she must have looked. The unexpected rain deluge had drenched her in seconds, and it was a miracle that some-one had offered to help. God knew how the rest of that day would have gone if the driver of the big SUV with a loud noisy family inside hadn't slowed to ask her if she needed help. Carrie, who unbeknownst to Jane had followed her out of the church, had arrived, breathless and dripping wet, while a tearful Jane was still trying to get her words out to the kind strangers.

The family had given the pair a lift to Carrie's flat, where Jane had poured out her story, or rather dripped it out, while they'd sat draped in towels drinking wine out of mugs.

'And you didn't tell Draco about this?' Carrie had asked.

Jane had shaken her head and did so now to disperse the memory. Why was she thinking about Draco so much lately? she asked herself crossly. Maybe it was becoming a mother to a motherless baby. The discovery that she wasn't able to become a mother had been the reason she had run away in the first place.

She'd thought about writing to explain, but what was the point? He would never forgive her for humiliating him. No, his only reaction would have been relief before the next long-legged glamorous beauty drifted into his life, and not for long. His love life had a built-in revolving door... Not that I'm judging, she told herself with a sniff.

If he'd had a lucky escape, so had she. Watching from a safe distance over the last four years, she had found it pretty obvious that, even if her inability to give him an heir had not been an unsurmountable obstacle, the marriage would not have worked. When she'd been in thrall to him, so desperately in love with the idea of being in love, the future had just been some rose-tinted, lovely place.

When she'd looked back she had been shocked to realise that virtually all their conversations, such as they had been, had involved her trying to say what he wanted to hear. It had never even crossed her mind that he might be unfaithful, and if it had she would have told herself that if he ever got bored with her it would be her fault.

The entire situation had been a disaster waiting to happen. She thought about it these days as skipping the middle bit and getting straight to the end, less pain and disillusion all around in the long run.

'Miss Smith.'

Jane blinked like a shocked baby owl as a reporter from a well-known nature programme appeared, backed by a cameraman.

Oh, God, she thought, pasting on a smile.

'You must be pleased about the turnout today.'

She took a deep breath. 'Pleased but not surprised that people care, that people are shocked and disturbed about this blatant act of environmental vandalism. Ten years ago a survey showed this area was home to four bat roosts, owls lived here and woodpeckers, and innumerable other wildlife have lost their homes. This is a protected habitat, there were tree preservation orders in place, the law was broken and for what? A quick buck!'

The reporter turned to camera. 'That was Jane Smith, who alerted the authorities to this incident.'

Jane gave a deep sigh of relief when the reporter still talking to camera smiled at her, mouthing thanks before he set a new course for the vicar.

'Oh, my, Henry is really enjoying his five minutes of fame,' his wife observed as she joined Jane.

'He's welcome to mine…that was terrifying… God, did I make a total fool of myself? How did he know my name?'

'You're famous—you kick-started this… As for making a fool of yourself, you were actually rather brilliant.

Oh, are you still on for book club or have you got another media gig…?'

Jane laughed and sought a firmer grip on her banner. 'Oh, I haven't read—'

'Oh, don't worry, neither has anyone else. Bring a bottle… No,' she mused, then glanced at Mattie, lowering her voice. 'Sorry, you'll be the responsible adult in the room, and don't worry, I'm not cooking,' she added, laughing to herself as she walked off.

Jane had never belonged to a community before. It was nice and at the same time desperately sad that the reason she did was because of a terrible tragedy.

Carrie should be here. Jane didn't want to be living a life that should be her friend's, even though it was a very nice life.

She still couldn't think about Carrie without the almost permanent lump in her throat swelling painfully. Carrie had come into Jane's life during her last year in the care system.

It had been the attraction of opposites. Carrie outspoken, and Jane, who had over the years in care perfected the art of fading into the background, but they had instantly bonded.

Then later, while she had been at art college, Carrie had found her lovely Robert and they'd married and had their baby, though not in that order. The weekend break had been their belated honeymoon and Jane had been trusted with their precious eight-week-old new baby while they were away.

'I wouldn't leave him with anyone but you,' Carrie had told her. 'Just three nights.'

Three nights had turned out to be for ever when the train the new parents had been travelling up to Scotland on had been derailed. Five months ago the tragedy had made the headlines every day, now it got the occasional footnote or personal interest story.

For Jane and Mattie it was never going to be a footnote. It had changed their lives for ever. Jane, who had never thought she would be a parent, was, or very nearly was. The official adoption was in the final stages, and she, a townie, was living in the tiny rural cottage that Robert and Carrie had inherited from his great-aunt.

Jane had been determined to adapt to rural living for Mattie's sake but, in the end, it hadn't been as difficult as she had anticipated. She had felt an immediate connection with the countryside, and had immersed herself in all it could offer, joining a rambling club, learning about foraging the hedgerows and woodland for ingredients for the weekly cookery classes given by a local chef in their village hall. She had been roped into picking litter from the village green with the local schoolchildren and spent an evening joining a guided bat-watch walk.

For the first time she understood the urge people felt to protect the countryside for future generations, for Mattie's generation. This was Mattie's home, his heritage, and the wanton destruction had made her react on a visceral, very personal level.

The sadness that hit her at intervals like a great black crushing wave settled on her shoulders and her placard lowered. Jane edged away. She needed a break and no one would miss her.

Then it happened!

During the interview she had been distantly aware in the periphery of her vision that a big sleek car was drawing attention, but not hers. She had never been into shiny cars. So her glance was incurious as it swivelled that way, no longer incurious when she identified the figure behind the wheel. Everything froze inside her, her breath hitched.

Dark eyes met and held her own… She was fighting for breath.

Her heart rate climbed.

She could hear the blood drum in her ears, so loud it drowned out the little cry of shock that left her parted lips.

It was him—Draco Andreas!

The memories flooded back, not a smooth flow, but a series of staccato images, from a time when she was infatuated by the idea of being in love. She had been blissfully oblivious to his fame and wealth or, for that matter, even the fact, initially, that London was not his home, but that he was there temporarily, for two months.

Back then, he was just Draco—the man who made her laugh, the one who seemed to genuinely care about her, not the CEO of Andreas Company, the man who was now renowned for changing his lovers the same way a normal person changed their socks.

Even his feet had been perfect!

Now that was a weird thing to remember, but it was a lot better than dwelling on perfect other bits!

The baby on her back woke, cried out, perhaps alerted by her tension, and began to fidget. She tightened her grip on the placard, sensed rather than heard the ripple of conversation trickle through the crowd as the tall, exclusive figure got out of the car.

Total mind-freezing panic bubbled up. This wasn't the moment for a confrontation.

That moment didn't exist!

With a quick furtive glance around, Jane seized the opportunity and was relieved when her legs obeyed the order and slipped away into the shadows of the trees.

As she distanced herself from the protest, the sounds faded into an indistinct hum. The familiar terrain of the untouched woodland welcomed her, the solace and peace it normally provided eluding her. It was a shock. She was fine. She just needed a moment—or maybe a year—to gather her thoughts, to reconcile that past with this present without gibbering.

Hands pressed against a moss-covered tree absorbing the texture, Jane closed her eyes. The gentle rustle of leaves and the distant murmur of the crowd might have created a soothing symphony, only it didn't.

Her thoughts were total and utter chaos. All she could think of was Draco's face—the golden toned skin drawn tight across sculpted razor-sharp cheekbones, a broad forehead and a strong firm jaw. The devil, it was said, was in the detail, but Draco had always made her think of a fallen angel, dark and devastating. The details of his symmetrical features were fascinating, mesmerising.

Her stomach muscles lurched as she dwelt on his deep-set midnight-dark eyes set beneath the thick bands of his brows and framed by dark, lush lashes. His carved cheekbones with their knife-sharp angles, dominant blade of a nose, contrasted in a dramatic, stomach-melting way with his mouth, sensual and full.

Authority clashing with sensuality and all utterly, totally male.

She clenched her soft jaw, refusing to be swept away by nostalgia, lust or longing, a weird combination of all three, and she was in no condition to analyse.

She just had to keep telling herself, for sanity's sake, that her life was different now, it centred around little Matthew and the responsibilities that came with guardianship. A gentler life with friendship and kindness, book clubs and village-hall yoga, which had its issues because she was the only person under sixty there— she couldn't include Maud, who had the flexibility of a ten-year-old.

With a determined breath, Jane steeled herself. Draco Andreas might be a part of her past, but she wouldn't let him disrupt the life she had built for herself and the child who depended on her. As she slipped further into the sanctuary of the trees, her thoughts circled around a decision—how to navigate the inevitable confrontation with the man who had once been the centre of her universe. He had surely either forgotten her existence or hated her.

Was it even inevitable?

Would she prefer he hated her than had forgotten her?

How would she play it?

Well, fancy seeing you here.

Oh, gosh, long time no see...

CHAPTER TWO

THERE WAS AN almost audible static hum of anticipation as the tall, dynamic Draco Andreas appeared, impeccably clad in a grey tailored suit and open-necked white shirt.

Jane was sitting in the back row behind a tall man with an even taller hat. She couldn't see the loose-limbed figure but she knew that he'd look perfect. She also knew that the eyes that would be scanning the crowd were more navy-black than brown-black, and his stare managed to give the person that came under their laser beam the impression that nothing was hidden from the owner.

The man in front whipped off his hat and she slunk down in her seat a little more. There were a couple of angry shouts and mutters that faded in the face of the effortless authority projected by the tall, lithe figure who, after walking up the short flight of wooden stairs to the small, raised stage, paused to shake the hand of the vicar before turning to his hostile but now silent audience.

He paused, seemingly perfectly at ease, his dark eyes scanning the faces turned to him, and despite being hidden Jane found herself instinctively shrinking back some more and lowering her lashes.

Not hiding? said the exasperated voice in her head. What else would you call it?

Pride had brought her here, the determination, after a lot of soul-searching, that she could not allow her blast from the past to derail her life.

Draco would leave her life as he had entered it, casually, and she must react in the same way. She wouldn't allow herself to run away or hide—both, to her shame, her initial instincts—but that didn't mean she had to advertise her presence.

For a board-wielding protestor, she really did have a genuine dislike of confrontation.

Would he even remember her?

She'd changed a lot in four years. When she looked in the mirror these days... When did she look in the mirror?

Juggling her job as a receptionist in the doctor's surgery and childcare didn't leave a lot of time for worrying about frown lines, and running around after a baby meant she had lost ten pounds she could probably not afford to. She knew that her face had lost some of its youthful roundness, and her last hair trim had been a nail-scissor bathroom-sink job...

Also her wardrobe was a long way from the designer clothes that Draco had bought for her. Bought and chosen... She was ashamed now of how malleable she'd been, how desperate she'd been to please him, how she'd allowed him to dress her up like a mannequin doll. She ran a hand over her hair, which he'd been fascinated by. He had gone so far as to extract a promise from her never to cut it; he always wanted to be able to wrap himself in it.

And she had agreed without a second thought.

There was nothing symbolic, she told herself, about the fact that she had lopped eight inches off her waist-length locks two weeks after the non-event wedding. It was just more convenient this way.

Unable to resist the temptation any longer, she bent her head to look around the man in front and saw Draco was still standing there, seemingly relaxed as he used his charismatic smile to obvious effect. She was not in the fainting zone of that smile, but she still felt the aftershocks of it.

Not recognise her? she mocked herself, retreating once more behind the grey hair, her heart thumping as she recalled that moment earlier when their glances had connected.

Draco had seen her and he had definitely recognised her.

She had read retribution in his face. Draco was not a forgiving man. Remembering his expression, she shivered, her overactive imagination conjuring up an ancient god about to do a lot of smiting!

Even if that smiting was in a twenty-first-century legal as opposed to lightning-bolt way, when you were Draco Andreas that could cause some damage!

Draco had recognised her, all right.

'Ladies and gentlemen,' Draco began, his lightly accented warm velvet voice awakening dormant interconnected nerve endings under Jane's skin in a tingly, painful way. 'Firstly I owe you an apology for the unauthorised tree-felling.' He paused to allow the big murmur to die down before continuing. 'I will not excuse what happened. There is no excuse. I understand your anger. I, too,' he declared sombrely, 'am angry.'

Someone beside her clapped and as Draco's eyes went to the spot and he smiled, everyone there thought he was smiling at them, but Jane was willing to bet that she was the only one whose stomach muscles were dipping and who had an embarrassing ache between her legs.

It was all she could do to stop herself yelling out, It wasn't me. I would never cheer you... Kiss, touch, taste—that was another matter!

She cleared her throat and reminded herself that all that wild, wanton behaviour was in the past.

The next part of his speech was lost on Jane. It took all her resources to resist the tug of the closed door and the freedom outside, freedom from the insidious sense-killing sound of his voice, and some increasingly disturbing thoughts about his mouth, which was beautiful and sensuous. He had a tongue that knew its way around... Stop that, Jane!

The entire section of his speech that passed over her head must have been good because this time the applause was more widespread. There were even a couple of grudging grunts of approval from a few of the most vocal critics, who had yesterday been calling for dire punishment to be visited on anyone that worked for his firm.

Draco had won them over. Always inevitable, she thought as she glanced around her at the rapt faces turned to the charismatic figure who now held them in the palm of his hand.

The way he had once held her breast in his hand, and in her head she heard his voice telling her it was the perfect size... She gave several sharp shakes of her head, took a deep breath and loosened her top where it chafed her painfully engorged nipples. Under the circumstances it seemed pretty pointless to pretend that the years had lessened her susceptibility to his male aura.

But fancying Draco Andreas hardly makes me unique!

Her lips twisted in a cynical, self-mocking little grimace as she glanced at the villagers. There had to be more than a few heads filled with fantasies involving the tall Italian billionaire, which was fine so long as they stayed fantasies. It was the common-sense-killing reality of falling for Draco that was dangerous.

Of course he had won over his audience; it was what he did. It seemed amazing now that when they had met, she hadn't known who he was. That fact had seemed to amuse Draco, and even when she had known the details she had still not taken on board the mind-boggling extent of his power, wealth and fame.

It was a measure of her infatuation and self-delusion that she had thought even for one insane moment she would have fitted into his life.

That she could make herself the sleek, elegant creature who drifted along at his side saying all the right things to all the right people.

The only way it could have worked was if she'd never opened her mouth, which would probably have suited

Draco. He had literally never spoken about his tech company or his role in the world of finance. Their conversations had revolved around the Tuscan estate, his face lighting with genuine enthusiasm as he'd described the place that was to be her home…the perfect place, he'd said, for bringing up children.

It was what she had wanted to hear, she thought sadly. He had been offering her what she had always longed for.

Refusing to acknowledge the pain that came with the thought, she told herself that she had her family now and it would be all the family she ever needed.

As for a man to complete her little family, she didn't think so. Mattie took up all her time and energy. As for sex, since Draco her libido had gone into hibernation and she wasn't about to wake it up, unless one day she was able to separate emotions from sex, and that she couldn't imagine.

She closed down the inner dialogue and tuned back in time to hear Draco say, 'I acknowledge that mistakes were made in the execution of our project.'

She risked another look and saw him spread his flattened palms wide in a *mea culpa* gesture. 'I take full responsibility, and I assure you that immediate steps will be taken, are being taken, to rectify the damage done to the woodland. A comprehensive tree-replanting scheme will tomorrow be initiated, ensuring the preservation of this beautiful ecosystem for generations to come.' Draco outlined his plans for environmental restitution before seamlessly shifting from the eco-project to community

welfare, revealing a grander vision that seemed to reso-
nate with the villagers.

You had to give it to the man, Jane thought, trying to
view his words objectively—and failing miserably—but
his delivery was sincere, if a little too slick. The cranky
addition made her feel a bit happier.

'I understand the importance of community,' Draco
said, his gaze sweeping across the faces before him.
'And in recognition of your patience and understanding, Andreas Company will fund the restoration of the
local church roof—a symbol of our commitment to the
well-being of this village.'

Nice touch, Jane admitted silently as a ripple of appreciation flowed through the hall. Draco Andreas, the
master of persuasion, was weaving a narrative that en-
deared him to the hearts of the villagers.

He hadn't needed to use his powers of persuasion to
get her into his bed, she recalled, her cheeks heating at
the memory of that first time, the look of shock on his
aroused, flushed face when he had realised he was her
first. She pushed the memory away and tuned back in
time to hear Draco say, 'As a further gesture of good-
will, I am extending an invitation to a member of this
community…' Draco announced, his eyes subtly searching the crowd.

Jane pulled back, shifted uneasily in her seat and felt
as if they had landed on her. Paranoia, she told herself,
looking at the grey hair of the man sitting in front of
her and channelling inner calm.

And failing miserably.

'We are hosting an alternative energy eco-train-ing course at my estate. I believe local representatives should be involved in shaping the future of green technology, and, after what has happened to your community and how you responded so robustly, I feel that your insights are invaluable.'

Jane felt the collective gaze of the villagers following as his stare turned towards her, and her chin lifted. This was not an accident.

As the villagers applauded, Jane pushed back her seat and got to her feet, throwing out a few smiling greetings as she made her way to the door with a couple of murmurs of 'Mattie'. Actually, her boss, the local GP who was also a neighbour, had said no need to hurry back when she had offered to babysit.

Jane made it as far as the gate before a voice calling her name made her turn reluctantly back.

'Vicar?' she said, politely waiting for the overweight and very well-meaning cleric to catch her up.

'Jane, dear, I'm glad I caught you. I did want to speak to you before but I was not expecting Mr Andreas to mention it tonight. I hope you don't mind, but when he told me about the course I thought of you. And when we discussed it at our meeting, so sorry you couldn't be there, but it was unanimous. Everyone agreed you'd be the perfect candidate—'

Jane cut him off with a laugh. 'Perfect? I can think of four locals who are a lot more qualified than me... actually more, because I'm not qualified at all.'

'But your enthusiasm and—'

'I am amateur hour and we both know it.'

The vicar looked momentarily flustered, but rallied.

'You started the ball rolling with our protests. You should be the one—'

Jane bit her lip. This was starting to feel like a conspiracy. 'Obviously I am very flattered you thought of me, but—' She bit back a sharp 'I'm not a charity case' and continued with a smile. 'It's out of the question, I'm afraid—'

'You are thinking about Mattie, but I understand there are crèche facilities at the conference, and a bit of Italian sun, a break, is just what you need, my dear.'

His comment confirmed her suspicion...poor single parent Jane could never afford a break in Italy. They meant well but the idea of charity made her hackles rise. 'I burn in the sun,' she said in a flat little voice.

The older man laughed as if she'd made a joke.

'Seriously. There are many more people better qualified than me for this...treat and the surgery is short-staffed.'

'Ah, yes, we discussed this with Dr Grace and she said you are owed holiday so that's no problem. She's already lined up a temp.'

Jane took a deep breath. She could see her avenues of escape closing. 'You seem to have thought of everything.'

'So you agree? I think it would be very helpful in setting up the exchange day with the inner-city school you suggested at the last parish council meeting.'

She sighed and thought, Me and my big mouth. On the other hand, take Draco out of the equation and it was tempting... But Draco was not the sort of man who vanished in a puff of smoke. His presence was not something you could ignore.

It was a mad idea, but she admitted there were temptations: the course would be interesting…and so would seeing Draco's home, his life… Yes, she was curious—who wouldn't be?

She still hesitated, but she was tempted.

Finally she gave a reluctant nod. It wasn't as if Draco would be a visible presence there. While it was great PR for him, she was confident it was the sort of thing that would be delegated.

'There would be conditions, obviously, with Mattie. I'd need more details.'

'Of course, of course, quite wise of you. I'll pass on your request to Mr Andreas.'

'Oh, I'm sure Mr Andreas has more important things to concern him. One of his many assistants will have what I need.'

'Thanks, but I won't,' Grace said when Jane offered her a coffee. 'And you know I love to babysit. I really miss the time when my two were small and didn't answer back—speaking of which, I need to check my lot have done their homework. As you know, they run rings around their dad,' she said with a roll of her eyes. 'You know, Jane, I am so glad you have agreed to Tuscany. You need a break.'

'It's not a holiday.'

'True, but I'm sure that you will find some time for a bit of sun and sea, maybe some down time with a good-looking Italian?' she teased before sweeping out, her ringing phone attached to her ear.

Jane shut the door, leaned back against the wall, closed her eyes and breathed out a gusty sigh. The only sound was the clock on the wall above the open fireplace. She'd have actually welcomed some angry baby cries at that moment if only to distract her from the thoughts swirling in her head.

She had levered herself off the wall when there was a knock on the door. Grace always left something behind.

Pasting on a smile, she pulled it open. 'What have you left this time?' she began.

Her smile wilted and her mouth opened as she raised her eyes a long way to the face of the man standing in her doorway, his dark head brushing the supporting beam of the open oak porch.

'Draco…! Mr Andreas,' she hastily corrected.

If his male aura had made her uncomfortable in the village hall, here she felt pummelled to tight-throated, heart-thudding, mind-emptying confusion by being this close to his unique brand of raw masculinity.

'Oh, make it Draco,' he drawled. The lift of one corner of his sensual mouth became a full mocking grin complete with flash of white teeth as he stared down at her from under his heavy-lidded dark eyes, the lashes so long they touched the razor-sharp contour of his cheekbones. 'I'm on first-name terms with almost all the women I've slept with, *cara.*'

His lazy mockery stung and jolted her free of her confusion—sometimes being angry was very mind-clearing, also it distracted you from thoughts of his mouth. 'And you remember all their names. I'm impressed,' she snapped back waspishly.

Draco took a mental step back. She was no longer trying to make herself invisible, a tactic that had always amused him—the adult equivalent of a child believing she had vanished if she closed her eyes—and now she was right up there in his face.

Did she actually believe that a flame-haired woman who looked like she did, with eyes like that…a body… He cut off the line of thought before it made an extremely uncomfortable situation even more painful.

He felt a surge of self-contempt, remembering how, in the days after she had humiliated him, he had lain awake at night and in between drinking, aching for her. Now he looked at her and admired the tilt of her nose, the wide-spaced, dramatically green eyes, the kissable lips, the stubborn tilt of her chin… A faint frown interrupted his self-congratulatory list. The stubborn chin—had it always been that way?

You can congratulate yourself as much as you like, Draco, but you're still hard as a rock, mocked the voice in his head.

An image of the bundled-up child on her back flashed into his head and the taunting inner voice helpfully pointed out, You won't be getting any, but someone else is.

This was a departure and not at all the way he had anticipated things going. The Jane he had known always had a warm sense of humour and a gorgeous laugh but sarcasm—that was a major divergence.

He studied her, admitting to his spark of curiosity but not his hunger as he took in the details of the soft contours of her heart-shaped face. Her big wide eyes, darkly fringed, looked back up at him, wariness shining in the shimmering depths, her mouth was still temptingly generous, but the angle of her rounded chin suggested a stubbornness he did not recognise.

As if anxious to dispel any impression that she'd been counting his lovers, Jane added haughtily, with a frown that knitted her feathery dark brows, 'Were you looking for me?'

He straightened up to his full, impressive, lithe and muscular six feet three and looked down at her, the flinty flecks like ice in his eyes and the mildness of his contempt making it all the more coruscating. 'Was I meant to look for you?'

Had she anticipated he would, and had she expected that reaction? Had she engineered this situation? The suspicion lingered, but she would have been disappointed. He had not chased after his fleeing bride. To do so would have made him his father—a man who had been so obsessed with a woman that it had broken him.

Obsessed to the point of insanity. In his father's case, his obsession had been the second wife he had left Draco's late mother for.

Antonio Andreas had indulged his second wife's every whim and all her whims involved money. And when the money to feed her appetite for luxury and excess had run out, and there were no more artworks for his father to sell, she'd predictably left him for someone able to give her what she wanted, leaving behind her young son, his half-brother, who would have cramped her style.

Without her around things could have got better—Draco had hoped they would—but they hadn't. His father, unwilling to accept the reality, had stalked his ex-wife online, and also in person on a number of excruciatingly embarrassing public occasions, begging her to come back to him.

He never seemed to lose his appetite to be humiliated, and, despite everything she had done, would never hear a bad word against her. When Draco, unable to hold back any longer, had spoken out, his teenage self had experienced not just the rough side of his father's tongue but his clenched fist.

Undoubtedly growing to despise his father had influenced his reaction to being dumped at the altar. The objective part of him recognised this. It had been a point of principle not to look for his runaway bride, not to allow himself to even ask why or where, let alone search for her.

And yet here she was. If he'd believed in fate he would have said it was meant to be, but Draco believed that a man made his own fate, not that he wouldn't take advantage of opportunities when they came his way.

Was this an opportunity? he asked himself.

If so, for what?

The revenge his anger craved?

Answers he wouldn't even admit to himself he needed? That he wanted to demand?

A guilty flush ran up under Jane's skin. She didn't pretend not to understand his reference and the double meaning—it wasn't the here and now he was referencing.

'No, I didn't expect that,' she said quietly, adding huskily, 'Why are you here?'

With his mouth lifted into a lazy, self-mocking half-smile, he asked himself the same question now.

To confront her, accuse her of engineering this situation?

Curiosity?

To see first-hand where she had chosen to live in preference to life with him and, he thought, staring past her, with whom…?

'Aren't you going to invite me in?' he asked her, even though it was obvious she wasn't. Maybe she was wondering how she would explain him to the boyfriend or husband? The father of her child, whose existence he still couldn't quite take on board.

'I—' Before she could think of an alternative to the blunt negative that she wanted to blurt, Draco, who was obviously not similarly inhibited by good manners, walked past her. It was a small space and Draco was not a small man.

Instinct made her close her eyes and try to make herself as small as possible, which was, she immediately realised, a pretty pointless exercise and not one that concealed the shameful fact the brush of his hard-muscled arm against her shoulder had sent deep ripples of desire through her entire body. The warm male scent of his body was lingering and making it hard for her to think clearly.

Loving Draco had always been insanity—wanting Draco, she corrected swiftly. The correction made it easier to breathe.

She might now know that marriage to Draco would have been a mistake and could never have lasted, but she was still scarily receptive to him physically.

Fact. Deal with it, Jane, she told herself, showing zero sympathy for this weakness.

How utterly and totally insane was it that she felt almost as bereft at that moment as she had that day she'd run away from the wedding?

Allowing herself a few calming hitches of breath, she turned and followed him into her small cosy sitting room, seeing the space through his eyes.

It didn't feel very cosy. Cosy and Draco? No, definitely not!

She nervously twisted her hands, her skittering gaze drifting around the room, anywhere, quite frankly, than at him. She saw the home that Carrie and Robert had lovingly built together, imagining how it might look through his eyes. Draco wouldn't see the items that had sentimental value, the repurposed thirties sideboard and the recovered rocker, he'd see cramped and slightly shabby.

The idea that he might be sneering made her skin prickle defensively. In the space of time it took her to pick up a toy that had fallen out of the toy box behind the sofa and replace it carefully her chin had gone up and she was able to face him with at least the illusion of confidence.

She had once been so sensitive to his moods that even the thought that she had said the wrong thing, worn the wrong outfit or used the wrong bloody fork would have felt like a failure, not good enough.

Well, this house was more than good enough and she would eat her food with her fingers and to hell with his distaste!

The moment the thought popped into her head she knew it was the wrong one because it brought with it the memory of an occasion when he had used his fingers to feed her a decadent creamy confection, she had sucked cream off his long brown fingers and— She stopped the destructive and criminally self-indulgent memory as she straightened up, one hand on her hip, her free forearm holding her hair back from her face as she delivered a look that said, Want to make something of the repurposed furniture? Because I will defend it with my life. She would defend every trivial detail of the home that had been made with love.

As their glances connected and held she had the satisfaction of seeing a startled expression slide across his lean features, followed by a slow speculative stare.

'I like what you have done to the place.'

Her eyes narrowed—he hadn't sounded sarcastic or sneery—but she only lowered her chin a fraction.

Draco could have done with lowering his head. It was almost grazing the low beams that Carrie had painted a warm shade of white to make the ceiling seem higher.

Her friend had laughed at the time, saying it was just as well her husband was short.

The memory brought a lump to Jane's throat and misted her eyes, and she blinked hard, not wanting to make an awkward situation worse by crying. It still happened at the most inopportune moments, the grief just bubbling up. She kept the moisture at bay through sheer force of will, determined not to look away.

White or not, the beams were not high, and Draco dominated any space, but the room's proportions made his presence even more overwhelming. It wasn't just a physical thing, not simply his size and sheer physicality, it was the restless energy he exuded.

He was not a relaxing person to be around.

Draco watched as she shook back her hair, which fell immediately into a fiery nimbus of bronze curls around her face and shoulders as she planted her hands on her narrow denim-covered hips and lifted her chin.

Jane took a steadying breath, hiding her grief behind a facade of defiant belligerence as she waited, determined she wouldn't be the one to break the silence.

She had to wait an uncomfortable length of time.

'You have changed,' he said finally, his eyes on her stubborn chin and the militant light in her incredible eyes. Never during their relationship had she been confrontational—in fact there had been times when her little shrug of acceptance, her placidity, had irritated him. The only time she'd shown fierceness had been in bed, which he hadn't objected to at all! There she had been fire to his dreams with her relentless fascination with his body and her utter lack of inhibitions.

She had never challenged him, she had never used tricks to manipulate him, unworldly to an almost unbelievable degree. Everything about her was the diametric opposite of his grasping, avaricious, conniving stepmother. She had never asked him for anything. In fact she had seemed uncomfortable with the gifts he had given her, politely grateful, but he had sensed her unease when he had filled a wardrobe with designer clothes.

Which made what she had done all the more incomprehensible!

Out of nowhere a memory surfaced, shaken loose perhaps by the perfume she was wearing now, the same perfume she had been wearing when she had pulled herself to her knees on the bed that was tumbled by their recent lovemaking and, pressing her small perfect breasts to his back, wound her slim arms around him and whispered that she loved him. Waiting, he knew, for him to return the sentiment.

Draco had not lied. He did not believe in love, love was the thing that had destroyed his father, but he thought he was gentle. The idea of hurting her had hit him on a level he had never recognised in himself previously or since.

He could remember with shocking clarity looking at the individual freckles on her smooth pale shoulder and breathing in the scent of her hair as he smoothed it off her graceful neck before burying his face in the silky softness.

'We are good together, cara. I can't get enough of you.'

She had smiled when he'd flipped her onto her back and begun to make love to her again, slow and languid this time. There had been sadness in her eyes, but he had pretended not to see it, ignoring the tickle of guilt, which now seemed ironic considering how things had ended.

Hearing the criticism in his voice, she assumed that he was referring to her recent weight loss and shrugged. Jane didn't find her jutting hip bones attractive or the sculpted prominence of her collarbones, so it was not really a surprise that he didn't either, but then her life no longer involved being the person that Draco wanted her to be.

Not now.

There was a freedom in that, she told herself. It made her feel strong…made her like herself, and she was a mother now. She was very conscious that a mother owed it to their child to like themselves, not to pass on their insecurities, teach by example… She had read all the parenting bibles, usually before she fell into a sleep of utter exhaustion.

If only she had had such self-insight four years ago. She had refused to recognise the flaws in their relationship, how unequal, how unhealthy it had been, until she was distant from it, and even then not until the pain of what had felt like a grieving process had passed.

'Actually I'm a perfectly healthy weight,' she countered, her lips tight.

He blinked. 'I didn't mean that,' he snapped back, sounding impatient at her interpretation. 'I meant… you…just seem…different…?'

'Well, it would be more surprising if I wasn't. It has been four years. You seem exactly the same,' she added, not making it sound like a compliment.

'I don't have a family.'

She nodded, thinking of the procession of girlfriends he did have as she watched him dig one hand into the pocket of his tailored trousers and look around, his gaze landing and lingering on the toys.

CHAPTER THREE

DRACO GAVE NOTHING away in his expression as he turned back to her and asked casually, 'Is the baby's father in the picture…?'

How long has he been in your life?

Is he the reason you walked out on me?

He couldn't voice those addendums without acknowledging how much he wanted to know and that was something he could not, would not do.

It came so out of the blue that Jane had no time to control her reaction. Her hand went to her quivering lips as she shook her head, seemingly unable for several moments to speak without breaking down.

Her discomfort, her stress was palpable. He'd be lying if he said he was displeased to sense some trouble in paradise.

Was the man married?

Had he cheated?

Or had he just not wanted the responsibility of fatherhood? Draco wondered, indulging in some speculation as he conjured up a man who was a total loser.

'Is it a joint-parenting situation?' How did that work? He never really had understood, but he supposed if people were willing to compromise for the sake of their off-spring... Personally he'd never been big on compromise.

Jane shook her head, not appearing to register the faint mockery in his voice. 'Mattie's father was brought up in the village,' she said quietly. 'He moved away then...he was a stonemason, a craftsman, an artisan. His little company was about to...' Her voice trailed away.

Draco felt his jaw tighten in response to her reverential tone then belatedly picked up on the tense.

'Was?' he queried.

'He died,' she said, her voice as dark as the bleakest dark winter night.

Her hand was covering her mouth again, the mouth that he had loved, the mouth that had driven him crazy as she'd explored every inch of his body. No sex had ever been like what he had experienced with Jane.

It was that sex and the mortal blow she had delivered to his pride, not loss, that had made the months after she ran away the toughest he had ever known.

He had got through it, and part of the joy of being rich was that he answered to no one. So if you holed up in a cabin in Alaska for two months, no one asked you why. Not even the guests at the wedding and definitely not the photographer with the images of the fleeing bride, photos that were now in Draco's possession.

It had seemed a fair exchange to Draco, and when faced with the choice he had offered the photographer had agreed.

'Publish and you will make money but I will ruin you.' Draco had not elaborated before he'd given the favoured option. 'Hand over all the copies, and I mean all, no insurance for your memoirs, and your career will go stratospheric.'

There had been rumours circulating, obviously, but no visual evidence and nobody willing to go on the record. He was known to be litigious, which came in handy. He doubted anyone had believed his 'mutual change of heart' press release, but no one had actually challenged it.

'I'm sorry,' he roughed out.

Her hand dropped, and her shimmering forest-green stare was disconcertingly direct, almost accusing, which, considering he was the injured party, was ironic.

'Are you?' His face was blank, which she had noticed when they were together was his way of dealing with emotional situations. She had always imagined that behind his mask were real feelings he could not articulate, but now she knew he hadn't said he loved her for the simple reason he didn't.

Draco said nothing.

What could he say? Moments before he'd welcomed the idea of her being unhappy. He felt a slug of guilt and thought, Be careful what you wish for Draco.

The pain in her eyes was… Unable to maintain eye contact, he turned his head sharply. Her vulnerability, her fragility shook loose feelings that were painful in their intensity, but he refused to name them.

'Were you married?'

She ran a hand across her face and gave an odd little laugh. 'No.'

'So being a single parent must be…'

'A learning curve,' she admitted, cutting in quickly. It wasn't a lie, it just wasn't the complete truth.

The silence stretched as he seemed to search for words, which had to be a first for Draco, as he glanced once more towards the toys.

'Do you have family close…?'

'I was brought up in care, Draco.'

The reminder brought the faintest of flushes to the slashing angle of his high cheekbones. 'I know that.'

'It just slipped your mind.' Because it hadn't been important enough for him to remember, she thought bitterly.

'I meant a support group… Your friend Carrie, was it?'

'It's a good community here,' Jane said quickly, not meeting his eyes in case he saw the tears shimmering there and biting down hard on her lip when she heard the quiver in her voice. 'The village is a good place to bring up a child. In a big town, a city, it must be harder. The villagers have been great. I think they suggested me for this course because they think I need a break, that, and the fact I brought the news crew here.' She took a deep breath. 'I can see how it might seem personal but it wasn't, though I think you're owed an—'

'An explanation?' he suggested helpfully.

Her eyelashes flickered against her cheek as her brain froze. She ought to have a practised response, but she didn't. 'No, I meant—' She paused, thinking, What did I mean? 'I meant you can blame me for your bad press but that doesn't mean I regret it, because I don't!'

'No, I don't blame you for the bad press. I blame the incompetent site manager who decided to cut corners. He is the reason I have had to make a detour to the back of beyond, but he won't be troubling you any longer,' he told her and watched her eyes widen. 'Don't look at me like that. I haven't put out a hit on him,' he said, sounding amused.

'I didn't think—' She broke off, a guilty unease settling over her. 'You sacked him?'

Jane had been vocal in her denunciation of the man. She had called him all the names under the sun when she had confronted him in the quagmire that had once been beautiful and tranquil, but despite that she took no pleasure from the idea of his ruin. What did she know? He might have children, a mortgage… She felt a stab of guilt at her part in the imaginary downfall building in her head.

Draco shook his head in seeming disbelief, watching the expressions drift across her face. 'I can't believe you feel sorry for the guy.'

'Not sorry, precisely,' she countered, lifting a hand to remove an annoying recalcitrant curl from her face.

Draco's eyes followed the action, focusing in on the fine-boned delicacy of her wrist, a delicacy that hid the supple strength of her body, lovely toned legs that could wrap tight around him, arms that could—

He tried to halt the memories but it was too late.

Heat he had zero control over was spreading through his body, flaring inside him as memories surged.

He remembered hearing the harsh rasp of her breath as he kissed his way down her spine, the little groans as her face dug into the pillow as he slid his hand between her legs, the fierce focus on her face when he entered her and—

One moment she was breathing, the next the air around them had become thick and heavy, making each breath an effort as their eyes locked, green on obsidian. Jane shivered as an illicit thrill of excitement spread though her body. Her entire world had narrowed to his dark stare. She felt as though the protective layers were being peeled away from her skin, leaving her exposed, but she couldn't break the contact.

'Draco…?'

It wasn't the slurred-sounding, bewildered warning in her voice that dragged him clear of the erotic spiral of memories. It was a sudden extraordinary, impossible thought as he recalled the excuses his incompetent employee had reeled out when he was trying to pass the buck. The woman he'd spoken of who had violently attacked him.

Jane realised she had been holding her breath. There was a gentle whoosh as she let it out and smoothed her hair back from her face. The dangerous thrum in the air had receded, leaving an awkwardness—at least on her part.

She rubbed her arms where the fine hairs were still standing on end as if she had just walked through an electrical storm, and silently called herself a fool. She'd been a foolish, starry-eyed virgin who had fancied herself in love the first time around. The second time... She caught herself up short, her eyes widening in horror at the dangerous direction of her thoughts—there would be no second time!

Five minutes in his company and she was already thinking in terms of inevitable, but nothing was inevitable except the fact there was no going back.

The sexual hum in the air had gone but Draco's stare remained unnervingly intense.

'What?' she snapped out, wondering if that breathless moment had been a figment of her imagination, the result of her hormones coming out of hibernation.

She dashed a hand across her small nose. 'Have I got something on my nose or something?'

Her comment drew his eyes to the light sprinkling of freckles across the bridge of her tip-tilted nose. 'Freckles,' he said, seeming lost in thought. 'Were you—?' he said abruptly before shaking his head and laughing. 'No...?'

'Was I what?' She stopped, gripped by a chill of horror. If he knew how close she had come to making a pass at him. Pass. It sounded so innocent when what she'd felt had not been innocent.

'Franco...the guy whose career you were so worried about.'

Her lips twisted in annoyance. 'Could you sound

more patronising if you tried?' Maybe he was trying. 'And,' she finished crossly, 'I was not worried. I am not about to lose any sleep over him!'

'It might make you feel better,' he continued, ignoring her intervention completely, 'if I tell you he tried to blame everyone else but himself.'

This had been a red line for Draco. The first quality required for good leadership was the recognition that the buck really did stop with you.

'Actually, one specific person who apparently was a foul-mouthed ranting witch who he suspected was not all there.' He tapped his own forehead to illustrate his meaning. 'She also physically threatened him…?' He paused. 'You…?'

'Not violence,' she protested. 'I was angry,' she admitted defiantly.

'It really was you. That is…?' He dragged a hand across his dark hair, making contact with a ceiling beam, and dropped it. Even after the confirmation it seemed barely credible to Draco, who couldn't equate the description with the meek, compliant woman he had once been engaged to.

'What a…'

He blinked as a word he had never thought to hear on her lips slipped out and she seemed oblivious to the fact.

'I ask you seriously—who wouldn't be angry? The heavy machinery had come in the night when we were all asleep. By the time I arrived the other men were drinking tea. It was a done deal. And he, that man, he had the cheek to tell me I was trespassing, which I wasn't. It was a public right of way. As for physically threatening him, I was holding the stick, I didn't use it.'

'You need a weapon for self-defence? I had no idea this was such a rough area.'

Her eyes narrowed in dislike. 'Bruce likes sticks. Bruce is a dog,' she clarified quickly. 'And he belongs to my neighbour. He'd slipped his leash and I was chasing him as I'm faster, and Grace took the pushchair for me. If that man is telling lies about me...'

'Relax, he won't be and he's been given a sabbatical... a long sabbatical.'

Draco blamed himself for the situation, hence his personal intervention. He despised the idea of neo babies being given a leg up the ladder, but he had personally signed off on this appointment, not because on paper the guy had the qualifications, which he did, but because Franco's father had promised apprenticeships to a dozen kids in his laboratory.

'Why didn't you think I was capable of it?' Jane demanded, finding relief from the maze of conflicting churning emotions in indignation. 'I'm capable of a lot more than you ever thought.'

'Yes, that was brought home to me the day you did your runaway bride stunt! If we'd been filming that would have gone viral because you come across really well on camera.'

'What do you mean?'

'Your interview earlier made the evening news bulletin.'

'Oh, God!' she said, horrified. 'You watched the coverage?'

'It was brought to my attention.'

'I thought billionaires didn't bother with the little stuff. They floated around on private jets and went to film premieres.' She stopped, thinking of his companions at the last glittering event he'd been pictured at.

'You wishing you'd stayed around to enjoy the lifestyle?' he mocked.

This first direct reference made her stiffen. 'I think we both know I'd have been a terrible wife for a billionaire. You still haven't said,' she added, 'what brings you here.'

'The eco-management course.'

'Oh, if it's oversubscribed, no problem at all.'

'It is not oversubscribed,' he retorted, framing the words with invisible quotation marks. 'I am led to believe you have...' He paused, his dark eyes glittering as they captured and held hers. 'Conditions?' He folded his hands across his chest, looking amused. 'I am here to hear them.'

Jane blinked in confusion. 'What?' Comprehension dawned. 'Oh, I didn't mean—!' Her shocked expression morphed into a frown. 'The vicar didn't say that, or mean that, and you,' she accused, 'knew it! I needed clarification of the childcare facilities. I'm not leaving Mattie with a stranger for hours on end. He needs continuity after...'

He arched a brow. 'After?' His eyes narrowed. 'Are there health issues?'

She shook her head. 'No, nothing like that. He is very young.'

'I have no experience of babies, but I hear they are very adaptable, but to ease your mind there will be several workshop situations that you can bring him along to,' he said glibly, hoping this was true and realising if it wasn't it ought to be. And not just because he had decided that having Jane within grabbing distance might be... Not that he would grab, he mentally corrected.

Why not? asked the voice in his head.

There was no denying there would be a sort of poetic justice in a role reversal. This time he would be the one to walk away...without an explanation.

No matter how many mental gymnastics he performed it was hard not to hear the word revenge. He was no saint, but he liked to think that taking advantage of a mother who had lost her partner was beneath him.

But it would be interesting to observe her reaction to what she had passed up on.

He wanted to see her regret...he wanted to know why.

He closed down that line of thought, not needing to admit what else he wanted and had wanted from the moment he had recognised her.

It was a weakness.

She was a weakness.

'I will send the prospectus and timetable of events.

No one is expected to attend them all, so there is time to spend with your son…there is flexibility.'

She felt a scratch of guilt. When she had seen him she'd assumed he had come here to…well, not be nice and certainly not show consideration. Clearly he had moved on, as, she reminded herself, had she, though not necessarily in the direction Draco thought.

Why hadn't she told him the truth about Mattie's parentage? she asked herself guiltily. His assumption would lead him to think she had moved on, which of course she had, but allowing the assumption to stand meant she didn't have to prove anything.

The guilt remained and she felt uneasy about the subterfuge. She hadn't planned this route; it had just opened up. She had actually assumed he already knew when he'd asked.

'Actually M…' The breath died in her throat when she looked up, the expression on his lean patrician features making her start to babble nervously

'Well, that is very…it sounds good,' she finished, her relief intense when he took the hint and began to move towards the door. 'Oh, w—'

Her warning was cut off as his head hit the low beam where Carrie had inserted the downlighters, the thump made by the collision of his skull with wood sending her stomach into a lurching dive.

Stunned, but not as stunned as he was, she watched with horror as he sank to his knees, his head on his chest. The slow trickle of blood brought her to her senses.

People said she was good in an emergency situation, but actually she just reacted.

She took a step towards him and fell to her knees beside him. 'Oh, my God, I should have warned you... I am...' Fewer words, Jane, said the practical voice in her head, and more action.

'I'm fine,' he muttered irritably.

'Don't be stupid. You are not fine.'

He looked at her through his fingers, which were already red. Luckily she wasn't squeamish. She was guessing it had been a long time since anyone had called him stupid.

'Sit down,' she coaxed, relieved when he managed to plonk himself down on the sagging sofa. She took hold of the hand he had clamped to his forehead. His healthy golden glow had an unhealthy pallid tinge and there were beads of sweat along his upper lip. 'Please don't go all macho and ridiculous... Let me see...'

She thought he was going to push her away, but he allowed her to thread her fingers into his thick dark hair, gently separating the strands to access the source of the trickle of blood that was dripping down his face.

'Here... No, that's the old scar...' she realised, exposing a long white ridge of scar tissue she had traced with her fingertips in the past. She had imagined him earning it doing something action-man and dangerous on the ski slopes.

And didn't that say everything there was to say about their relationship? She had never asked and he had never volunteered the information.

'Here it is...quite deep. You might need stitches.'

'I won't need stitches.'

She glanced at his face. His colour was a lot better. 'If you say so…but unless you want to look like some gory advert for a horror film, you'll let me help. It's self-interest,' she added. 'I don't want to be known as the woman who attacked a billionaire.'

His dark eyes swivelled her way. 'Just the woman who left him standing at the altar.'

Jane froze.

She had half anticipated that the label would follow her for the rest of her life, but it hadn't. Miraculously there had been no photos on social media, maybe because phones had been banned at the wedding, something she had thought a bit over the top at the time.

Her eyes slid from his and the challenge in them— this was not the time or the place for explanations and she doubted there ever would be a right time. If he knew her reasons, he'd be relieved, which she could cope with, but his pity… No, she really couldn't take that.

'I will get something to…' She made a vague gesture and got to her feet.

When she returned carrying a bowl of water and the contents of her first-aid box, Draco was still sitting on her sofa, looking more normal apart from the blood.

'Send me any bills for the furniture.'

She rolled her eyes. 'There is no blood on the furniture.' Plenty on his shirt and a few blobs on the polished wooden floor. 'Lucky I'm not squeamish,' she observed prosaically as she laid the bowl on the restored carpenter's chest that served as a coffee table. 'This might hurt,' she added, trying to sound chattily indifferent when she really wasn't while dipping a cotton swab into the water where antiseptic swirled.

Objectivity was really hard to fake when she was this close to his hard, lean male body, when a thousand memories, tactile and visual, were flitting through her head, and her stomach was performing somersaults as a hunger she only allowed to surface in her dreams dug in, painfully real.

'It's not actually as deep as I thought,' she admitted, her frowning regard on the clean wound where the copious flow of blood had reduced to a steady seep. 'You might not need stitches,' she conceded, taking a deep breath. If nothing else, the act of asking would prove she had moved on. 'But this other scar, that must have been...'

'A skull fracture, which, as I'm sure you're thinking, explains a lot.'

Jane wasn't laughing. He could feel the empathy coming off her in waves.

CHAPTER FOUR

'HOW DID THAT HAPPEN?' This time she didn't need a deep breath; the question came naturally.

'I fell while I was…' He had told the story so many times. Including to the medical staff when he had arrived in the emergency room, but somehow the words wouldn't come now. 'My father punched me. I fell and hit my head on a…'

He stopped. It was the expression on her face that brought home to him what he was doing… Which was what, Draco?

He was not a sharer.

He did not require sympathy or, worse still, pity, so why the hell had he just told Jane a fact that he had never told anyone?

'It was a long time ago and I was an extremely irritating kid.'

Jane sucked in a breath through flared nostrils. She knew that Draco's father was dead, that his only close relative was a half-brother, a lovely skinny beanpole of a boy who she had met briefly the day before the wedding, but in that moment she hated that father with a teeth-clenching passion.

Her small hands clenched into fists of outrage until the words bubbling up inside her could not be contained and they escaped in a rush.

'He beat you?' she cried, disbelief and outrage throbbing in her voice.

Draco had regretted sharing the moment he'd opened his mouth, but he hadn't been anticipating her dramatic reaction.

'I had a late growth spurt, so not after that occasion.' He'd been safe from his father's increasingly dangerous mood swings. His father had not been the sort of man who would hit out at someone who could hit back. But he had been the sort of man who would hit someone smaller, so Draco had delayed starting university to make sure that the same didn't happen to his little brother. 'He drank himself into an early grave.' And Draco never had made it to university. He didn't feel the loss.

'Good!' she exploded, then caught his expression and refused to back down. 'I'm sorry how that sounds but, well, I hate bullies!' she hissed. Appropriate or not, her emotions could not be contained.

Draco contemplated her fierce expression, the sparking defiance in her green eyes, the hectic flush on her smooth cheeks, and found it hard to believe that he had once considered her a gentle, mild creature outside the bedroom.

The bride he had imagined would create no dramas. Except, of course, her exit from his life had hardly been without drama, he reminded himself drily.

Catching her full lower lip between her teeth, she

lowered her gaze and looked at him through the mesh of her dark lashes. 'I'm sorry if you don't like that, but there it is.'

'I wasn't too keen on him either,' Draco responded lightly after a long contemplative moment.

Jane didn't respond. She was struggling with all her strength to escape the hypnotic tug of his dark stare until she reached the point where the necessity to do so didn't seem so urgent, despite the warning bells ringing in her head.

'I always assumed that you had a happy childhood,' she mused, sounding confused as she settled back on her heels beside the sofa. They had been engaged to be married and they had never come close to sharing as much as they had now, when they were nothing to one another.

She shook her head against that deeply bleak thought and, pushing her hair back from her face, tangled her slim fingers in the glossy skein.

She didn't mean to bring up the elephant in the room; it just happened as she blurted, 'Why did you ask me to marry you, Draco?'

Draco's response was equally uncensored. 'I wanted to keep you in my bed for ever.' How long before she had been in another man's bed, the man who had given her a child? The question left him with an odd hollow feeling.

A solitary tear began to trickle down her smooth cheek as he watched, releasing an emotion that he refused to give a name to. He inhaled as it broke loose in his chest, creating a suffocating feeling.

Was she crying for her dead lover, the father of her child?

He leapt to his feet explosively, frustration etched into his lean features.

Jane chose the same moment to get to her feet, and, clumsy in her haste, she almost knocked the first-aid box over. At least it distracted her from the shameful fact that her sensitive pelvic muscles had gone into quivering spasm.

Their impetuous actions had brought them face to face.

Her breath hitched as he caught her face between his big hands and bent his dark head. She saw a glimpse of the hunger in his eyes and refused to allow her heavy lids to close. She would not surrender her control.

The alternative to losing control was taking charge, so she did. Bringing herself up on her tiptoes, she placed her hands around his face, feeling the rasp of light stubble, and she took control, fitting her lips to his.

For a split second he did nothing as he inhaled her scent and then he was kissing her back with a blind, relentless, consuming hunger. Little husky sounds of desperation escaped her throat and were lost in his mouth as the combative contact grew rougher and less disciplined, all heat and hunger.

Then it was over and they were looking at each other—glazed shock duplicated... She saw the moment the shutters came down in his black eyes and decided it was a good thing.

The last thing she wanted was some sort of postmortem, not that the frustration thrumming through her body needed much analysis.

Draco had always been able to turn her into a person she hardly recognised. It had once felt like freedom; now it felt like loss.

'Well, that was stupid.'

She never allowed herself to wonder what would have happened if her doctor's appointment had fallen after they had married, because she knew. His life since then had proved he was a man who played the field and got bored quickly.

She was aching for something that had never existed, which made her angry, mostly at herself. He had never said he loved her, just that he wanted her, and by now that lust would have turned to boredom. Idiot, she chided herself, focusing on the reality, which was that he had lost no time replacing her in his bed and she was no longer the woman who was seduced by a man telling her he needed her, he wanted her... Even if that man did have a voice that ought, if there was any justice, to be illegal.

'Pleasurably stupid.' He looked down. She barely came up to his shoulder, so fierce, so hot, she did more with a kiss than he had ever imagined possible. 'That's why I proposed, *cara*.'

In other words, just sex.

It was really hard at that moment to remember that she needed more than sex. Actually she didn't even need sex; she needed a quiet, neatly ordered life.

Draco and neat and ordered were a contradiction in terms.

'Oxymoron,' she said out loud, then fielded his quizzical look with a shrug. 'I'd be flattered if it weren't for the fact that your version of for ever, according to what

I have read, is about a month,' she said, taking refuge from the ache inside her in the not very pretty truth.

If she hadn't been such a besotted innocent she would have realised at the time that a highly sexed man like Draco, a man who had women throwing themselves at him, would never have been satisfied with one woman.

'The wedding...it wasn't planned. I never intended...' she began before her voice trailed away. 'Just think about all the money you saved on a divorce,' she completed with a laugh that had a fake, hollow sound even to her own ears.

'You signed a pretty tight prenup.'

'Oh, God, so I did. I'd forgotten about that!' It had not been important. She hadn't even read it.

'You think I would have cheated on you?'

Unbelievably he sounded angry. 'Call it a wild guess,' she shot back.

Her anger faded into something far more complex as she watched his eyes drift from her face to her heaving breasts, or actually maybe not so complex, in fact totally basic. She had not kissed another man, let alone had him touch her, since her aborted wedding day.

After the first few months of her existing in a limbo state between misery and more misery, a medical emergency had broken the cycle of despair.

Her endometriosis had flared up, and the acute attack, with pain on another level from the chronic discomfort she had grown accustomed to, had hospitalised her.

As luck would have it, the hospital had been making a push to lower its gynaecological waiting lists and paying private clinics to slash the queues.

Jane had found herself part of this scheme and transferred to a clinic where her keyhole laparoscopy had been performed the very next day. Just in time, the surgeon had said. High on painkillers at the time, she hadn't asked, Just in time for what? And later she hadn't wanted to know.

The procedure to remove the plaques that had been causing her so much pain had been a success, though she had been warned that this was not a cure and in the future a hysterectomy might be the only solution left to her.

Jane had decided not to think too far ahead. This was a reprieve and she had no intention of not taking advantage of it. Cure or not, without the chronic pain her life was changed and for the better. She felt as if she'd been given a second chance—if not to have her own children, then she could work with them.

Her job at the care home had been on a zero-hour contract but that had not been an issue and there were never zero hours in the understaffed sector. The flexibility had meant she could fit in her hours around her pre-nursing college course, the first step on her way to fulfil her new ambition to be a children's nurse.

She'd had a purpose again.

But so much for plans—they were as fleeting as happy endings. Her life had changed again when there had been the knock on the door and the terrible news. She knew she would never be the mother that Carrie would have been, but she was damned sure she was going to try.

She was a mother now and there was no room in her

life for the chaos that came with Draco, even had that particular door been open.

'I think you should go. Shall I call someone for you?' she asked, glancing at his head.

'I'm fine.'

Mattie chose that moment to wake and his angry shout drifted down the stairs.

'Your son?'

'Matthew... Mattie...'

'How old?'

'He's seven months. He was eight weeks when...'

He watched the look of loss spread across her face and it hit him. The eight weeks she spoke of, or couldn't, was when the baby's father had died.

'If you'll excuse me... I should go.'

He gave a quick tip of his dark head and without another word was gone. Jane leaned back against the door, her hand pressed to her lips. I kissed him!

The shame was mingled with an illicit thrill of excitement. Her body was still tingling from his touch, and just thinking about the hard imprint of his aroused body sent a pulse of heat through her pelvis.

She breathed slow and deep, trying to gather her scattered senses, then Mattie yelled and, reminded of her priorities, she felt a sharp stab of guilt and flew up the stairs.

Jane almost forgot the printout of her itinerary for the next three weeks and turned back to the cottage to grab it off the table, pushing it into her carry-on bag.

She knew the departure and arrival times, but the

details had not included the airline she was travelling on. When she had emailed a request the person she was corresponding with had told her she would be met at the airport with tickets and further details.

She had decided that, rather than book a transfer, it would be more economical to hire a car, which would be waiting for her when she arrived at the rather obscure Italian airport. Her satnav had given her a route that appeared to avoid any major built-up areas and suggested it would take her two hours to get there.

'You've got everything this time?' Grace teased as she got in the car. Mattie was already ensconced in the back seat next to Grace's teenage daughter, who was great with him.

'Definitely sorry about that, but you wouldn't believe what a nightmare it is packing for a baby.'

Grace laughed and nodded to the rear-seat passenger. 'Oh, I would, and it doesn't get any better, I promise you. This one always wants to take her entire wardrobe,' she joked, ignoring the indignant 'Mum' from the back seat.

'Nervous?' Grace asked as they drove along.

Realising she was chewing her fingernails, a horrible habit she had kicked ages ago, Jane gave a self-conscious grimace and hastily withdrew them, glancing at her neat, clear-polished nails before putting them firmly in her lap.

'I've never been to Italy before.' It seemed strange to think that she had once been planning on spending the rest of her life there. She hadn't even considered how difficult that would be or suggested that she accompany Draco on one of his overnight trips home. Her level of acceptance now seemed bizarre to her. 'And I've never been here.' Jane looked around curiously. It felt different from any airport she had been to. There was no parking issue, for starters, and they pulled right into a space outside a small terminal building. 'I've never heard of it before.'

'I've never been here either, but a friend did their flying course from here and obviously I've never been in a private jet.'

'Private jet!'

Grace looked amused by her horrified expression. 'Didn't you realise? Want to get your pilot's licence or need a stop-off point from your end-of-the-garden helicopter pad, this is your go-to airport. It avoids the congestion over London.'

'But I'm not booked on a private jet.' Her initial confidence wavered as she saw a suited figure approaching the car, flanked by two women who looked corporately slick.

Grace unfastened her seat belt.

'Looks like you have bagged the company jet, lucky you!' her friend said, nodding to the logo on the side of the jet on the runway.

Jane followed the direction of her friend's stare while in the back the youngster bounced excitedly and pleaded, 'Send us loads of photos for me to post.'

'Oh, God, no!'

From the back seat the teen piped up, 'How is this bad?' before a glare from her mum reduced her to silence.

Sensing her friend's horror, Grace said cheerily, 'I

think you'll find you are. It'll be a fantastic opportunity to meet some of the others on the course ahead of time, scope out the talent,' she suggested with a mock leer.

'Mum…?' This time the reproach came with a giggle.

Jane rolled her eyes, but asked herself if it would be so bad to discover someone nice and normal, not to mention safe, to have some fun with. An image inserted itself in her head of someone who was neither nice nor normal, and as for safe!

'I have no time for men. I have Mattie.' Jane almost choked at the way her prim response sounded, but it was true, and a lot better than admitting Draco was a hard, no, impossible act to follow. Because he made you so happy, mocked the ironic voice in her head.

'Being a mum is not like taking the veil, Jane.'

'Oh, God, gross, Mum!' the teen in the back seat responded, covering her hands with her ears.

'I know things didn't work out for you last time.'

Jane sighed. She really regretted that extra glass of wine at book club, but at least her confidences had stopped at, 'I was engaged once—it didn't work out.'

It was a bit disorienting to have the reception party not only help unload her luggage but coo over Mattie and stay with her as she moved smoothly through Customs.

Wow, she thought as they settled in their seats in the empty cabin, this was travelling, but not as she knew it! She glanced through the window, wondering when the other passengers were going to board. Was she early?

It wasn't until they were in the air that the penny dropped: there were no other passengers!

She was confused. Had other people cancelled, or

was this Draco showing her what she had missed by not marrying him?

There was no doubt it was a comfortable way to travel, especially with a baby, who lapped up all the attention from the cabin crew who pronounced him beautiful, but, and she knew it was probably irrational, she felt resentful.

She felt as though she were a puppet who no one had bothered to consult, so no change there. Don't ask, just lavish luxury and she will stay in her box!

But Jane was no longer happy in her box! And she couldn't wait for an opportunity to prove it.

The transfer at the other end was equally smooth. There was no juggling baggage, no issues at all until she was shown the waiting limo.

This was an opportunity with neon sign directions.

The entourage that had followed her exchanged glances and looked nonplussed and alarmed when she shook her head and told them, channelling polite but firm, 'I've got a hire car. I'm driving myself.'

This was a cue for a lot of ultra-alarmed looks and some waving of hands, which, when she stuck to her guns, eventually became helpless Latin shrugs tinged by worry.

It struck Jane as a big fuss about nothing.

'Right, Mattie, let's do this!' she said with false jollity when she got behind the wheel of what the online details had described as a compact hatchback.

Compact was generous and the way the person handing over the car had sternly told her that any damage would incur severe penalties seemed a bit over the top, considering the number of dents and dings in the paintwork.

She also found and disposed of several crisp packets and a crushed soft drink can under her seat, which maybe explained the incredibly low price of the hire. Still, so long as it got her there and it wasn't far. She took comfort from the logistics.

Though not far in miles, the road was scary—there, she'd admitted it—and had to have doubled the distance.

There were several times during the journey when she regretted her decision to refuse the taxi service offered, especially when she had to pull over on a really lonely road to change Mattie's nappy and feed him, glancing over her shoulder at every shadow and sound. When Mattie had subsided, replete, her supply of food exhausted, Jane found herself hoping that the stock of baby food offered by the organisers was more realistic than the description of the hire car.

If not, she was in serious trouble!

The satnav, while accurate and indispensable, had chosen the shortest route, but maybe, she began to realise, not the easiest one.

Of course, the views were incredible, or they seemed that way on the rare occasions she took her eyes off the road for a split second. Those occasions were few and far between because she really didn't fancy driving off the edge of a mountain or ending up in a ditch.

Talk about white-knuckle ride!

When Jane saw the first sign bearing the name of her destination she gave a sigh of relief and felt some of the tension edge out of her rigid, aching shoulders. By the time she reached the massive wrought-iron gates that took her off the public highway she had passed three more signs and the tension was back.

At least when she'd been focused on not driving off a cliff she hadn't been thinking about what would happen when she did arrive, and now she was.

She drove towards the huge, elaborate gates wondering what you did to get inside—ring a bell?

There were no bells that she could see and it all seemed rather grand. Was there a trade entrance?

'Oh!' She actually leapt in her seat then laughed at herself as the gates silently opened. Of course, there were cameras, she thought, trying not to imagine the anonymous eyes watching her as she drove through and began the last leg of her journey.

If this was a driveway, it was not what she thought of as one. She had driven a good half-mile along a mercifully bump-free road through dense forest when the sunken lights alongside the verge burst into life, illuminating the road ahead and revealing an area of manicured parkland with the blue shadowed mountain to one side and the sparkle of sea to the other.

'Oh, wow!' she breathed and she cranked down the window a crack to inhale the salt and pine scent of the air.

It became less a breath and more a gasp when the palazzo came into view. Obviously she had looked it up but the generic photos online did not come close to the full open-mouth impact of this first glimpse, even though she hadn't been expecting a small cottage. But this… The sheer scale of the building standing before her made a statement—presumably something along the lines of 'We are rich and powerful! Do not mess with us!'

If so, it communicated the message well!

Set against the backdrop of dark sea and the first streaks of crimson from the setting sun, it made that statement even more dramatic.

She took in the symmetrical rows of deep identical windows on three levels, the huge baroque porticoed entrance and the impressive sweep of steps that shone white in the fading light.

Would she get a chance to see inside?

This was where Draco had said they would bring up their children. The recollection seemed even more surreal now she was seeing the place, though only as a visitor.

She hesitated, taking her foot off the accelerator as she approached a fork in the road. One quite obviously led up to the house; the other she presumed led to the buildings she could just about make out behind the distant bank of trees and shrubbery.

She had turned the wheel to head away from the palazzo when the figure stepped out of nowhere…one minute there was no one there, the next he was there.

CHAPTER FIVE

JANE SLAMMED HER foot on the brake and closed her eyes, anticipating a thud.

When she opened them, Draco was standing there making her think of some sort of glowering gladiator, a bare inch between him and the bumper of her car. Typical of the man, she thought, still shaking with reaction that he had not even bothered to jump out of the way. Startled, she glanced at Mattie in his car seat, blowing bubbles, oblivious to the near miss.

Her heart contracted with love for him.

Draco strode around the side of the car, his face like thunder, wrenched the door open, and stood there, waiting.

She had seen Draco annoyed before, irritable, and even in a bad temper, but she had never seen him really, really mad. It was an awesome sight in the way a hurricane was awesome, but you still didn't want to be in its path.

She could think of two ways to deal with this—well, three if you counted turning the car around and getting the hell out of there.

Jane didn't count it.

So that left being placatory and apologetic, even if she didn't know what she had to apologise for, or going on the offensive.

She hummed softly to herself, embracing the spirit of rebellion bubbling up inside her as she exited the car and stood there blinking up at him while easing the crick in her back.

Her stomach flipped. She accepted it as inevitable. Only Draco could look as gorgeous with his hair standing up in spikes where he had dragged his fingers through it. He looked very large, very angry and quite desperately beautiful, wearing a black shirt and trousers. His expression made grim look light-hearted.

'I wasn't expecting a reception committee,' she tossed out audaciously and saw his eyes narrow. Weirdly, she got a bit of a kick out of winding him up. 'You look…' her lashes lowered momentarily '…not happy? Sorry—am I late?' she wondered perkily.

'Late?' Her entire attitude was provocative, from the little smile on her pink full lips to the toss of her head.

His temper hit the red zone as he made one last attempt to contain it and then let rip.

Jane stood there and heard him out, waiting in the post-explosion silence before she responded, not in an effort to be provocative, just to get her breath. Nothing on her face showed the heart-thudding effect his diatribe had had on her—he really was awesome.

'You finished?' She watched his nostrils flare as he exhaled and opened his mouth. 'Before you say anything else, it might be a good idea to switch to English.

I have not the faintest clue what you just said to me… sorry, *yelled at* me.'

They had planned for her to take an immersive course in Italian after they had married. Draco had begun the lessons in the bedroom, introducing a vocabulary she doubted any language tutor would have offered.

The shameful pulsing throb between her legs made her voice sharp as she continued.

'If you greet everyone this way I can't imagine anyone coming back for a return visit. Your bullying might be acceptable for people who work for you, but I don't!'

'Bullying?' he echoed in insulted disbelief.

She could imagine that women didn't talk to him that way, or, for that matter, anyone, but tough, she decided, enjoying the feeling of rebellion.

'I am not a bully!'

'You yell at people who can't yell back. Well, that is no longer me!'

'I do not yell at anyone, and I never yelled at you!' he countered, clearly outraged at the accusation.

'You didn't have to. I agreed with everything you said!' she pointed out bitterly.

'Because I make good sense, because I always had your best interests at heart.'

'You believe that? Then you're even more arrogant than I thought.'

A look of self-conscious unease drifted across his face before his jaw tightened. 'My temper got the better of me.' The concession appeared to be dragged out of him against his will. 'But that is hardly surprising!'

* * *

He had spent the last hour plagued by images of smashed cars at the bottom of cliffs, broken bodies, the lick of flames. No wonder he had lost it, but at least she hadn't understood what he had said.

'If you thought I was going to run you over, I thought I was going to run you over, which was much worse.'

'You think this is about you driving like a lunatic?' He dismissed the idea with an expressive Latin gesture.

'I do not drive like a lunatic. I happen to be a very good driver! If I wasn't a very good driver I would have hit you. Also, I was driving at a snail's pace. But I get,' she conceded, 'that it must have been scary for you.'

He looked at her in utter astonishment. 'You really think I yelled at you because of that!'

She shrugged. 'I haven't been here long enough to make you mad about anything else.'

'You disregarded my instructions for your transfer.'

Instructions. Now that really grated. 'Oh, my God, you really are a control freak. Your office sends out a memo and if it's not followed to the letter you freak out!'

The provocative sound of her mocking laughter set his teeth on edge. 'I presume you were trying to prove a point, though what point I can't begin to imagine.'

'I was not!' She just resisted the impulse to stamp her foot because that would not help the mature and adult high ground she was determined to inhabit.

'So you flouted my wishes, the arrangement I put in place for your and the baby's comfort—'

'You put it in place… Seriously, Draco, you expect

me to believe that you even knew what arrangements had been put in place?'

He ignored the sarcastic intervention. To respond would have involved addressing the fact he had been personally involved in all the details of the arrangements for today.

'It is three and a half hours since I received the information that you and the baby were not in the limo sent for your safe transfer,' he said, emphasising the safe. 'I was informed that you were driving yourself in a cut-price hire car!'

'That's just like you, to judge everything on its value.'

'I'm judging it on its brakes, which does not seem unreasonable. Your actions seem at best childish. I have no experience of what travelling with an infant involves but I am pretty sure that it is not relaxing. Your behaviour would have been mildly irritating had this happened in England on roads you are familiar with, but this is very much not England. The more secure route here would have taken you three hours, the shortcut offered by your satnav two and a half.'

Her guilty expression said it all.

'Have you any idea how many accidents have occurred on that road, how many foolish tourists have come to harm?'

She flinched but maintained a defiant attitude as he hammered the point home.

'All right, it was not a good road.'

The concession didn't cut any ice with Draco, who had spent the last two hours thinking of those blind corners and hairpin bends, his imagination going into overdrive.

He had been first at the scene of a crash the previous month when luckily no one had been seriously injured, and the guy at the wheel of the horsebox should have known better.

Draco knew every twist and turn, every blind corner like the back of his hand; he had cut his teeth and honed his driving skills in this terrain, but even he only used the shortcut in daylight hours, and then in a four-wheel drive.

'You could have been caught out there in the dark.' A fact that had lain heavy with him as he'd waited, feeling totally impotent, and as he'd watched the sun begin to sink, his anxiety had turned to cold fury.

He never second-guessed his decisions but he had regretted his decision not to drive out and intercept her. She could have taken the sensible longer road and there were several points on both routes where the driver had an option—the chances of him missing her were high. For all he knew she could have recently passed her driving test. He didn't have a clue as he had never asked her.

What had he asked her?

You were never that interested in her life story, were you, Draco?

He pushed the tickle of guilt away. He had remembered that she was brought up in care, and he could recall thinking it meant that there would be no embarrassing relatives coming out of the woodwork.

His anger didn't dissipate but it was now diluted by a guilty awareness he was reluctant to acknowledge.

'I arranged for you to be brought here. Why did you not come as arranged?'

Her chin went up. 'Arranged?' She shook her head, making her curls bounce then settle into soft golden coils. 'I did not ask you to make arrangements for me, and I was not included in those decisions. I am very sorry that you have been inconvenienced,' she said with an insincere smile. 'But I had made my own arrangements.'

She watched as a look that on anyone else she would have called bewilderment slid across his lean features. His stabbing gesture was all frustration, before he dragged a hand across his already ruffled dark hair.

'You rented this...' Lips curled in contempt, he launched a vicious kick at the car wheel. 'I do not think much of your arrangements.'

'Do you mind? I have to pay for any damage.'

'I'd pay to get it towed away and crushed. You thought a child would be safe in this!'

The fact that Jane had thought the same thing numerous times during the journey made her respond to his comment even more indignantly.

'How dare you?' she snapped, her eyes flashing green fire. 'My parenting skills are not your business, and at least I don't assume throwing money at a problem is all it takes to solve it!' she huffed contemptuously. 'You can stick your limousines up—' Her eyes widened as she came to a breath-hitching pause. 'I just want to say...'

What do you want to say, Jane?

'I am not your problem and,' she added defiantly, 'I really don't think I'd take advice from someone whose idea of parenting is holding your girlfriend's lap dog while she pouts for the camera.'

His expression moved from fury to blank astonishment before melting into a grin that made it hard to stay angry, actually hard to stay on her feet.

'The thing bit me,' he recalled. 'I had to have a tetanus shot.'

As the tension dissolved Jane covered her mouth with her hand to smother an almost-laugh. She was only partially successful. 'Good!' she growled back.

'I am discovering that size is not a measure of combativeness,' he observed as he studied her face and wondered how it was possible he had never seen or even guessed at this fire in her personality. 'I was concerned.'

'Why?'

The question was so wilfully stupid that he had to wonder if she was going out of her way to provoke him, but he would rise above it, he decided. 'The road I am assuming that you took is not for... Before you explode once more, even locals take the longer route.'

'It wasn't a nice journey,' she admitted, allowing herself to be slightly mollified. 'But if there was a car organised this end you should have discussed it, or,' she corrected very quickly, because she didn't want him to think she had expected personal treatment, though this did seem pretty personal, 'have someone discuss it with me.' All her communications thus far had come via the office of Draco Andreas. And once the image from a sixties spoof of someone gorgeous with endless legs and red lips sitting on his knee taking dictation had got into her head, it had been impossible to banish.

It was there now as she said coldly, 'I require options, not ultimatums. I am quite capable of organising my own life and making my own decisions.'

'So I am seeing,' he observed, studying the obstinate set of her round chin.

'Look, obviously—' she sniffed contemptuously '—you think I couldn't find my way out of a paper bag. But I'm really not that helpless.'

Draco, his expression indecipherable, looked at the small finger being waved at him.

'All right, I am sorry if I put you out, but...' It suddenly occurred to her he had made special arrangements for her... And more troubling, if that was the case, why? Maybe he just thought she was hopeless and—

Pressing her hands together and closing her eyes briefly, she called a halt to the flow of disjointed question marks in her head and took a deep breath. 'It's been a long day and I understand there is an induction session early tomorrow, so if there is someone to show me to our room, Mattie—'

On cue the baby began to wail.

Draco watched as she ran around to the passenger door of the car. Something in her expression as she bent over the baby seat and spoke soothingly to the sobbing child before she picked him up in her arms made things tighten painfully in his chest.

The cries lessened to a dull roar as she walked back around the car towards him. 'Just point me in the right direction.'

'There has been a change in the schedule. Because

not everyone was able to make it on time it was decided that tomorrow will be a free day.'

Jane tried to hide her relief behind a smile but she knew she failed. 'Oh, that's…good to know. Is it far to the—?'

She glanced towards the spread of buildings, their roofs at different levels hidden by the trees, able to make out lights in the gathering gloom.

'Not far, but you are not in the annexe, though if you decide to attend the meet-and-greet supper there later tonight someone will be on hand to escort you.'

A meet-and-greet supper! Perfect to top off the journey from hell and a near-miss collision. Opting out sounded very good to her at that moment. 'Not… I must have misunderstood. So where are we staying?'

'The centre does not have adequate childcare facilities. We have allocated you rooms in the main house.'

Jane listened to the slick explanation in silence, her wide eyes swivelling to the palazzo. The sun had almost sunk and in the semi-darkness it was now lit by spotlights.

'Is there room?' she asked and laughed, even though she didn't really feel like laughing. It was strange to know that once she had been destined to be mistress of the place. She would have arrived here as a bride, not a visitor… She took a deep breath. The point was it hadn't happened.

'Right, okay, where should I…?' Her glance moved from the baby who was nuzzling her neck to the car. Mattie would kick up a hell of a fuss now if she tried to put him back in his car seat.

'I could drive…' Draco looked at the car, imagined the discomfort of fitting his legs into the front seat and decided. 'We will walk,' he announced, showing what she considered an uncharacteristically sensitive appreciation of her dilemma. Or maybe he just fancied a stroll.

'Someone will bring the…car,' he announced, with the confidence of someone who knew there were always people to do his bidding. 'And your luggage. I will show you the way.'

Half down the incline, Draco paused. 'He looks heavy.'

'He's a big boy,' Jane agreed. 'Oh, my goodness, the gardens…' She stared in wonder at the vision stretched out before her. Strategically placed spotlights revealed a series of terraces descending down the steep incline overlooking the sea to one side and the green plain on the other. The terraces appeared to be connected by gates and stairways, and the water from an ornate fountain spilled down the interconnecting levels, ending in a pool in the main terrace outside the palazzo.

'It is quite nice,' Draco agreed, then, with a grin, added, 'English understatement. It rubbed off in school.'

He had never said, but Jane had always had the impression that Draco's English school experience had not been a good one. He had always said that he would not send their children away to school.

The children they never could have had.

'Was his father tall?' Draco kept his voice carefully neutral. A dead man would be a difficult rival for someone who wanted to take his place.

Luckily Draco did not, but he wanted to know, he thought he deserved to know, if this man was the reason that she had walked away from the altar. Had they already met? Had she realised that she needed to be with this man…that nothing else mattered?

'No, but…' Jane stopped. Carrie had been tall and athletically broad-shouldered, her sparkling eyes and way of looking at the world projecting confidence and hiding her vulnerability. An image of her friend the day she had told Jane she was pregnant drifted into Jane's head, the snatch of conversation playing.

'I don't know how a real family works,' Carrie had confided in a panicked whisper.

Jane, who had been given up for adoption at birth, was equally ignorant of the dynamics. She had never found her for ever home. She'd been on the brink of adoption twice. The first time the mother in the family had become pregnant and they had decided they didn't want Jane. The second time she had felt for a short time as if she was part of a family, but before the adoption had been signed off the husband had been diagnosed with a chronic muscle-wasting disease. There had been tears on both sides when Jane had been sent back to the children's home, but she knew she had been loved and that was something no one could take away from her.

'A real family works on love and you and Rob have enough to spare, don't you think?'

Sometimes you said the wrong thing and others the right thing and this had definitely been one of the latter. She remembered her friend's expression clearing.

'We do, don't we? And he or she will have you for an aunty so that's lucky too.'

Jane's arms tightened around the baby as she hid her face in his soft wispy curls of baby-soft hair for a moment.

'I didn't mean to upset you.' The gruff self-recrimination in his voice made her pause mid-step.

Jane raised her eyes to his face as she took the opportunity to hitch the baby into a slightly more secure position on her shoulder and wished she had not packed away the baby sling, which would have left her hands free.

'You didn't.'

Her swimming eyes said otherwise.

Draco's glance shifted from her face to the baby she held, but the unfamiliar and unwelcome feelings sliding through him did not ease. 'I should take him.'

The abrupt announcement drew a startled round-eyed stare from Jane. 'You?'

She looked almost as shocked to hear him make the offer as he had been himself. The idea of holding something so small and breakable filled him with more horror than a market crash!

He nodded and shrugged. 'Why not?'

How hard could it be?

'But—'

Her reluctance served to harden his resolve. 'There are a lot of steps and it is dark; you can't see your own feet carrying the baby.'

He watched her little grimace of acknowledgment as she pulled the baby in closer, her chin resting on his head.

'I should have driven you down...' But this was one

of the best views of the palazzo and he had wanted to see her reaction. He winced at the insight.

He had wanted to see her regret when she saw what she had walked away from. In the end, though, she had walked away from him, and his ego wouldn't allow him to admit that this inescapable fact still hurt.

'Well, thank you, but the gardens are lovely. I can't wait to see them in daylight.' The light had almost faded completely now, though the path was well lit, and she got a sense of the garden. 'It smells gorgeous. Thank you...' she husked again as Draco bent forward, arms outreached to take the baby from her. She held her breath but still felt her senses thrum when the warm scent of his skin tickled her nose.

'Yep, perfect,' she praised.

Jane lowered her gaze, for some reason she didn't delve too deeply into, the sight of him standing there with Mattie in his arms. The contrast of big man and tiny baby, made her throat tighten with emotion.

'My mother replanted this area many years ago.' Her startled gaze lifted in time to catch the softening around his mouth, the warmth in his eyes, which a moment later vanished as the iron hardness reappeared as if a switch had been flicked and he provided unemotional additional information. 'I tried to reinstate the planting exactly as it was as a memorial to her.'

'That's a nice thing to do.' It suddenly struck her how strange this was, to be standing here talking this way.

When they had been together Draco had never discussed his family much, and when he had it was mostly information about his younger half-brother's achievements. His late father he'd never spoken of at all, she didn't have any idea when he had died, and the only time he had mentioned his mother it had been bare, bleak, bone-dry facts.

His parents had divorced and she'd died a year later.

When Jane had offered sympathy he had closed the conversation down, leaving her in no doubt that the subject was a no-go area—there had been a lot of those.

Jane had wanted to probe but never asked questions back then, had told herself that he would confide in her when he needed to. Now, of course, she knew he never would have.

Their relationship, certainly from his side, had never been about talking or sharing; it had been about sex. Maybe they were talking because they were no longer a couple. They were no longer having mind-numbing, incredible sex... Even then, when she had been so invested in being with him, she had sometimes wondered what, beyond the sex, was keeping them together.

She shook away the thoughts in her head, annoyed with herself for reading anything significant into a casual comment, for making it something more than it was.

Ah, well, the 'keep out' signs no longer applied to her. She wasn't the fiancée trying to say the right thing. Now she could say the normal thing. If he didn't like it, it no longer mattered, she told herself, wanting to distance herself as far as she could from the woman she had been.

'Did you go with her, your mother, when your parents split up?' She half expected him to tell her it was none of her business but, rather to her surprise, after a pause he responded.

'He wouldn't let her take me. And once Jamie was born, I couldn't have left him anyway.'

Jane felt a stab of frustration when he stopped talking. She remembered that feeling of being kept on the outside all too well. His expression was hidden from her by his long, luxuriant lashes, but she'd already seen the regret in the dark depths, presumably that he had told her even this much.

She felt a wave of self-disgust, hardly able to believe that she had meekly accepted his lack of communication as the norm when they were meant to be in a relationship.

'I remember Jamie,' she said, thinking of the stick-thin shy thirteen-year-old she had been introduced to the night before the wedding.

'You made a big impression on him,' Draco said drily, remembering his brother's accusing eyes when he had demanded to know what Draco had done to make her run away.

'How old were you when your parents divorced?'

'Fifteen.'

'So that would have made Jamie…?'

'He was born a month after they married. Watch your step. There's a…' With the hand that wasn't supporting the baby, he caught her elbow as she stepped off into space, or at least six unexpected inches, and landed with a jolt.

'Thanks…sorry, I wasn't looking where I was going.'

No, she'd been looking at him. There was no doubt

he was well worth looking at, no point denying the glaringly obvious, and the stubble that was now darkening his cheeks and jawline added an extra earthy… Do not think earthy, Jane, she told herself firmly. She could not allow this to drift towards the obsession she had once felt. No, he was just a good-looking man—okay, a gorgeous man—she had once had a relationship with.

If only he'd let go of her elbow!

How many erogenous zones could there possibly be in an elbow, for God's sake?

'He must be getting heavy. Shall I take him back?' Extending her arms enabled her to escape the skin-peeling contact of his hand and shake off his grip on her elbow without it looking too obvious.

Draco slung her an amused sardonic look. 'Thanks for the offer but I think I'll manage.' The baby was not his issue. His inability to stop staring at her lips was.

CHAPTER SIX

THE BABY OBLIGINGLY let out a howl of anger and, red-faced, started kicking and squirming, which focused Draco's attention on the angry bundle.

'What did I do…?'

Her lips twitched as she watched Draco, none of his habitual 'master of all he surveyed' cool written on his face. Instead there was something that on anyone else you might have called panic.

'Nothing, he's hungry. Let me take him back.'

This time he didn't argue, just muttered something in Italian as the baby was passed between them with no drama, if you discounted the shivers that slithered down her neck where Draco's warm breath brushed her sensitised skin.

Jane began jiggling the baby in her arms. 'Nearly there,' she hushed softly as they reached the lower terrace of the gardens that fed onto the wide stone area in front of the palazzo itself.

The baby responded to her voice and the decibels reduced. 'You are nursing?'

He didn't appear uncomfortable asking the question, but Jane could feel the heat climb up her neck until her face was burning with colour, not because she was embarrassed, but because she felt guilty.

Here was yet another chance to fill him in on the facts. It wasn't as if it were a guilty secret or, for that matter, a secret at all.

Of course, she had a secret, but there was no reason to share it with him. 'No, I'm not feeding him myself.'

'I understand it is not always so easy.'

He understood? The suggestion that he had researched breastfeeding issues might have made her laugh had she not been holding a fretful baby.

'Ah, here is Livia.'

If he sounded relieved, Jane felt a million times more so.

'Livia will show you to your apartments.' He turned to the other woman, who was wearing a dark trouser suit and what Jane rather uncharitably interpreted as an intense eager-to-please expression. She ought to know—she had worn it herself once upon a time.

'This way, please, Miss Smith. I hope your journey was not tiring?'

With a charming smile the woman stepped aside to allow Jane to precede her though the massive ornately carved double doors.

It was like walking into another world. She stood and her head dropped back, taking in the ceiling that appeared to float miles above her head. Works of art adorned the gilded and stuccoed areas of the walls, the remaining walls covered, not in plaster, but with massive mirrors painted with laurel leaves.

Classic sculptures, busts of women with Roman profiles and alabaster faces, stood on the plinths that ran down each side of the massive entrance leading up to a dramatic carved staircase. Marble again like the floor, it swept up to the first-floor gallery where it split, drawing the eye up to the glass dome high above.

Amidst all the classicism was the furniture, large and dramatic pieces, all vibrant colour and ultra-modern clean lines. Two massive sofas beneath the classic plinths were emerald green and the towering steel-framed bookcase a striking red.

Jane stared, not taking in a fraction of the detail.

The other woman, who smiled and stood silent, seemed to understand her awe.

'They made many discoveries during the restoration, but I am sure you do not want a guided tour just now. You are this way.'

She led Jane down a corridor lined with ancient statuary and works of art to a door that opened to reveal a lift, which was not at all ancient. It took them to another floor in smooth seconds, which Jane was glad of. She never had been keen on enclosed spaces.

This corridor was lined with windows that must make it very light in the daytime, but at the moment it was lit by low-voltage lights in the sconces that lined the opposite wall.

'You are here.' She opened the door and waited as Jane stepped inside, not to a bedroom, but to a large living area. The furniture was modern but not statement pieces, just high-quality craftsman-made matching the walls that were painted in a pale plaster colour.

'Oh, do not be concerned,' she said, seeing the direc-

tion of Jane's gaze. 'The balcony is childproof.' She nodded to the row of doors. 'Not that that is an issue at his
age,' she added with a smile. 'There is a small kitchen.'
She pushed open a door and Jane had the impression
of white and glossy. 'The other doors are the bedroom
and nursery, which interconnect, and the bathroom is
shared. I hope this is suitable? There is also one off the
playroom, should you wish to use it, but possibly he is
not that age yet.'

Jane watched as she opened a door to reveal a bright
yellow-painted room that looked like any child's idea
of paradise. There was a series of cartoon characters
painted on one wall, shelves containing neat stacks of
boxes and books on another. The low table with chairs
in the middle of the room was empty, but she could
picture it littered with toys from the boxes distributed
around the room. She imagined a child sitting on the
wooden rocking horse.

A child with Draco's dark hair and eyes.

She turned away, a lump in her throat, and began to
jiggle Mattie up and down in her arms.

'You're right. I don't think this one will be making
use of those facilities…' She heard the door close and
was glad.

'Shall I get someone to unpack for you?' The other
woman nodded to the luggage stacked in the corner,
which Jane had not previously noticed.

Draco's airy confidence that her car would be dealt
with seemed justified as her luggage had arrived before she had. She picked up the folded buggy and, with

a practised flick of her wrist, unfolded it one-handed before placing Mattie in.

'No, that's fine,' she said, clipping the safety harness. 'I'll unpack myself.' There was not much to unpack. Mattie's things took up most of her luggage allowance. 'This is absolutely…well…' she swept a hand in an expressive gesture around the room '…perfect, but I think,' she began hesitantly, 'that there might be some mistake?' she suggested, feeling the need to double-check. 'I am here for the conference. I'm not a house guest. I am meant to be in the—' She began to feel in her pockets for the course details.

'Mr Andreas did not consider the accommodation there suitable for an infant.' The woman glanced fondly at Mattie, who was stuffing one chubby fist in his mouth, a very serious expression on his face. 'My nephew is his age. He is a very pretty baby too. Oh, the fridge is filled with the formula you requested and some basics for yourself.'

Jane had considered that a nice thoughtful touch when she had filled in the online form. It had saved her a lot of luggage space.

'Thank you,' she said, absolutely overwhelmed by the kindness being shown. 'I feel I'm getting preferential treatment,' she admitted guiltily.

'Not at all. I understand the evening meetings might go on late and it was decided that these apartments will be more suitable, much quieter, less disruption.'

Jane acknowledged a sense of relief. People said nice things about babies, but when it came to a good night's sleep they were less tolerant, and who could blame them? She had pictured sitting down to breakfast with a lot of unfriendly stares directed her way from heavy-eyed sleep-deprived people.

Here Mattie was not likely to bother anyone but her and she had adapted quite well to disturbed sleep patterns. As for the evening meetings, she doubted she would make many.

'It's…' She paused, torn. On the one hand she felt guilty because this did not align with her egalitarian principles, but on the other she was so happy that everything was geared to her and Mattie to a degree she could never have dreamt of. 'Sorry, I'm repeating myself, but this really is perfect.'

Perfect, but an enigma, a perfect nursery, what did she know? This was not her world. Maybe that was how billionaires did it, put in a nursery in case a guest had a baby. Maybe it really was as simple as asking a chef to offer a vegan option.

Or maybe it was something even simpler—this suite of rooms was historically a nursery and no one had thought to change the function when the place was restored, they'd just updated the decor and the facilities? Was it possible that Draco and his brother had occupied the rooms?

An image of a youthful Draco flashed before her eyes, along with the possibly false idea she had that his childhood had not been that happy and it was more than a broken-family scenario. She was overthinking this—just thinking about Draco was overthinking!

When she had agreed to this, she had told herself that,

beyond some rousing introductory speech, she would not have to see Draco.

Did you really think that or were you hoping…? She would not even allow the question to form.

The scenario she had imagined involved her seated at the back of a room clapping politely along with the others.

The older woman beamed and, seeming to understand Jane's unposed question, but not that she was fighting the pain of loss with every fibre of her being, added in a confidential undertone, 'I was not here at the time, but I believe this was the old nursery and intended to be so again when…' A self-conscious look spread across Livia's smooth face as she paused, straightened the snowy collar of her white shirt and added, with the forced professional air of someone who realised she had said too much, 'The staff still speak of it. It was a sad time here.'

Jane froze…sad time. Could the woman be referring to the aftermath of her runaway bride act? She felt a slither of unease. Obviously she knew she had made the right decision, but she had been so busy dealing with her own emotions in the aftermath that she hadn't thought about the possibility of a knock-on effect for people she had never met.

She knew that Draco had been angry…but she also knew that his heart had not been affected. How could it have been? She had never had his heart. His ego was another matter.

'I am sure there will be babies here one day.' The comment was delivered with an accompanying confidential smile. 'And in the meantime it has come in useful for you.'

There will be babies!

Just not mine.

'It's really lovely. I'm grateful. I'll have an explore, before I bathe Mattie.' She smiled, hoping the other woman recognised the not so subtle code for 'I want to be alone'.

She really did! The entire day had been exhausting and then the cherry on top, just when she ought to have been recovering after the drive from hell, she had walked straight into Draco, or driven into, and a little too literally for her liking.

He didn't seem to have registered that she could have killed him... Even thinking about that moment made her stomach quiver violently.

Draco was the most alive person she had ever encountered...loved... That she no longer was in love with him did not alter the fact that the idea of him not being in the world was a possibility she simply couldn't accept.

'Should you wish anything...'

I wish to stop thinking about Draco.

In which case coming here was not such a great idea.

'I'm fine,' she said brightly.

To Jane's relief the woman appeared to be moving towards the door and she politely mirrored the action. 'Thank you so much.'

Alone at last, she thought, looking around the room. Focusing her thoughts on the practical and away from the dangerous, she decided to leave the bags and prioritise settling Mattie down. He took his feed well. He became animated in the bath, kicking and splashing, but as she dried him and put him in his sleep suit she could see his eyes were growing heavy. She rocked him on her shoulder, crooning softly until she felt his little body relax into sleep.

She tucked him up carefully in his cot and tiptoed out of the room, leaving the door ajar.

Despite her attempts to dismiss the woman's comments, the words continued to ricochet around in Jane's head as she stood in the nursery that was furnished for the children she and Draco would never have.

Though he would have children—the housekeeper had implied as much. Had the comment been code for Draco having plans to marry? Pressing a protective hand to her stomach, Jane felt her eyes fill with tears... She dashed them away angrily.

She returned to the nursery to check on Mattie, her heart swelling with protective love as she stared down at his flushed sleeping face. Making her way back to the small but well-equipped kitchen, she cleared away the things she had used to make the feed and pushed back the chair she had pulled over to feed him. Through the open window the light breeze blew in the scent of lavender mingled with the salty tang of pine.

She should not be feeling nostalgia or regret. She should feel relieved that things had never reached the point where she had to tell Draco she couldn't have children.

That was one nightmare scenario she had avoided, and so had he. The sentence drifted into her head.

I am sure there will be babies here one day.

She closed the window with a snap and, though the entire place was wired for sound, went back to check on Mattie, who was still fast asleep, snoring softly.

Smiling, she blew him a kiss and banged her head on the butterfly mobile above the cot.

Unpacking her own things did not take long as Mattie's clothes had taken up most of the case. Of course now she knew she could have brought several cases.

She looked at the few lonely items hanging in the cavernous wardrobe. She stood there wondering what happened now.

She knew that to appear suitably keen good manners meant she ought to go to the informal supper, but he had suggested it was optional, and there was no way she would drag Mattie out. Delaying the moment when she was revealed as a phoney appealed at that moment.

Although she was starving.

She was wondering if there was anything in the fridge besides formula to stave off the hunger pangs when a tap on the door drowned out the sound of her growling stomach.

The girl on the other side introduced herself. 'I am Val, the nursery nurse. Well, not really. I help my brother with the bees.'

'Right,' said Jane, amused by the girl's intensity, confused by the mention of bees, and impressed by her excellent English. 'But when guests need a babysitter I help out. I have plenty of experience. I have five smaller brothers. I am here to sit with the little one should you wish me to, though if you prefer not to go for supper it will be delivered here.'

'I...' Jane hesitated and stepped aside for the girl to enter. 'Please come in. Mattie is asleep and normally he sleeps for several hours after his evening feed.'

'Oh, that is so lucky!' Val exclaimed chattily. 'My youngest brother still wakes twice in the night!'

'Look, it's very considerate of you to offer.' Jane paused, realising that it was unlikely the girl had volunteered—this was her job. 'I'm not dressed.' Jane, feeling creased and grubby after the journey, gestured down at her jeans and shirt, thinking that even if she was 'dressed' it would not be very impressive.

'No problem. Even if you don't want to go down to supper I could stay while you shower?'

'I'd probably hear Mattie, but actually that would be great,' Jane admitted, smiling her gratitude. It would be a treat to have a shower without listening out for Mattie.

'Supper is being served at seven-thirty?'

Val saw Jane's face and grinned. 'I don't think it will be a late night—there are a lot of old men with beards.' She looked self-conscious. 'Sorry, that was rude. I quite like beards.'

Jane laughed and the girl looked reassured. 'No problem if you want to take it here.'

The shower, with its array of bewildering controls, was twice the size of the entire bathroom in her cottage...actually, her bedroom. As Jane revolved in the pummel of the warm spray she could feel the knots in her neck and shoulders begin to loosen and she allowed herself the indulgence of enjoying the luxury.

She couldn't remember the last time she'd lingered in the shower and there had not been any long, luxurious soaks in a long time.

When she finally forced herself to leave, she felt, if not a new woman, certainly a less tense one. Encased in one of the mountain of fluffy robes, she returned to the bedroom after first glancing in on Mattie, who was fast asleep.

Maybe she would skip supper and just have a glass of milk. Half an hour earlier she'd been starving but now her appetite had gone. She was often so busy that she rarely sat down to a meal, instead eating a sandwich or something on the go. Some days she went to bed and realised she'd forgotten to eat; it was an effort to drag herself out of bed to make a sandwich or have a glass of milk but she made herself—mostly.

If she hadn't the clothes hanging in the wardrobe would look even more ill-fitting than they already did, she thought, putting her travel-creased clothes in a linen hamper and trying not to catch sight of herself in the full-length mirror.

The packet of online information on the course had said there were laundry facilities, which was a relief and a must when you were travelling with a baby, so Jane wasn't really worried about the negligible wardrobe, which took up a couple of hangers and one drawer.

She hastily selected some fresh underclothes, a denim cotton skirt, which, like many of her clothes, felt too loose at the waist, and a sleeveless blouse, pale blue with splurges of orange, that tied at her midriff. She fastened it with a knot but it still gaped sightly, showing a sliver of her midriff. The shirt looked like silk but wasn't, hence the bargain price.

Dragging a quick comb through her hair, she shoved her feet into a pair of sandals and hurried back to the sitting room, where the young girl was looking at her phone. When Jane entered she put it back into her pocket.

'I have decided not to go to the supper,' she said immediately.

'Of course, I will have some supper sent up to you.'

'Actually just a sandwich... Have you eaten? Am I keeping you from your supper?'

'Oh, I've already eaten. There are always sandwiches, salads and so forth laid out for staff on duty during the evening.' She pulled an apple from her pocket like a magician.

'That sounds perfect. Give me directions and I'll go and help myself if you don't mind sitting with Mattie?'

'I don't mind, but you're a guest.' The girl looked doubtful.

'Really, I could do with stretching my legs and getting my bearings before tomorrow. Just direct me to the kitchen.'

'Well, there is a back way that is much quicker—the elevator at the end of the corridor, not the one you came up in. Turn right out the door and just walk to the end. You can't miss. It will take you directly there.'

'I won't be long, and if Mattie wakes...' She pulled out her phone and gave the young woman her number.

'Can't miss it' were, in Jane's opinion, classic famous last words, but actually she didn't miss it and a short while later found herself, not in the main kitchen, but in what appeared to be an anteroom where food was laid along a long table. There was plenty of food left but the room was empty.

There was much more available than sandwiches and salads under their plastic coverings, including a few warm dishes in a heated trolley, which Jane avoided. By now she had totally passed the point of being hungry but recognised she needed food.

With some smoked-salmon sandwiches on a plate, she had intended to go straight back to the nursery, but as she walked past a stable-style door, its top section open to allow the gentle breeze to enter the room, she paused, filled with a sudden longing to breathe in some of that sweet-smelling air.

Carefully unlatching the bottom, she closed it after her and stepped outside into what appeared to be a courtyard. Several storeys rose above it. None of the windows were lit; they just seemed like black empty eyes looking down at her.

There was nothing sinister about the central area, which, as far as she could tell, was a neatly tended kitchen garden, which explained the fragrance that had brought her outside. At the far end there was a tall stone arch, and moonlight filtered through.

Standing curiously in the opening, she was transfixed by the view of the moonlit gardens, the gentle trickle of flowing water from the series of fountains blending with the not so distant hush of waves retreating on a shoreline she could not see.

Without intending to, she found herself wandering

along one of the paved pathways bordered by lavender that brushed her legs, filling the evening air with perfume as she glanced back to check that the arch was still in sight. She didn't want to lose her point of reference and get lost.

She laughed under her breath, a bitter sound. She'd already lost her way the moment Draco had stepped back into her life. Something about him seemed to disable her ability to think straight, to make rational decisions.

'I'm beginning to think this was a bad idea, coming here. Beginning?' she mocked, looking around the magical setting and huffing a small ironic laugh. Who was she kidding? She had always known it was a bad idea.

But I came anyway.

She had told herself it was a logical choice, that she had been left with no option, but the reality was she could have said no at any point. She could have wriggled out of it, but she hadn't.

'Why?' she asked herself, before closing her eyes as if she could block the answer to her question.

Draco was like a drug. She had gone cold turkey to get him out of her system and it had hurt. She really couldn't let him back in.

Telling herself fiercely that she wouldn't, she didn't register the toe of her sandal had caught in an uneven ridge in the paving until she had left it behind.

With a muttered curse of frustration, she turned back to retrieve it just as the moon slipped behind a cloud.

The sudden darkness was so profound that it was as

if someone had switched a light off. She stood stock-still and waited for her eyes to adjust to the light or, rather, lack of it.

CHAPTER SEVEN

THEY DIDN'T NEED to adjust. The moon reappeared, re-vealing the enchanting gardens and the fact she was no longer alone.

Her heart took a plunging dive before climbing into her throat, a helpless primitive shiver of awareness slith-ering down her spine, and she shivered, too shocked to even attempt to retreat. As if her secret thoughts had summoned him, Draco, the real flesh and blood one as opposed to the one in her head, was standing there a few feet away holding a wine bottle in one hand and her sandal in the other.

'Is this where I see if the slipper fits?'

She took a step towards him and snatched it out of his fingers… For a second he didn't release his grip. What was infinitely more disturbing was that for a second Jane didn't want him to.

Balancing on one leg, she slid her foot back into the sandal, not taking her eyes off him the way you didn't take your eyes off a dangerous jungle cat about to lunge.

You should be so lucky, mocked the voice in her head.

Though the analogy was not so far out. There was something quite…combustible about him, she decided, her eyes going from the bottle in his hand to his face again as she marvelled at the perfect symmetry of his features that were all dark shadow and light relief, like a starkly beautiful pencil sketch, his shadowed jaw adding to the edgy vibe.

'What are you doing here?' she began in a cranky voice that made his dark brows lift sardonically. 'That is, it's your home, of course you're here,' she said quickly, glad the shadows hid her embarrassed blush. 'I just assumed you would be at the meet-and-greet supper.'

'Me being the host?'

She nodded and he followed the direction of her gaze to the uncorked bottle in his hand. 'The trick of good management is delegation, and I thought you'd be there.'

'Looks like we were both wrong,' she said, struggling to stop her gaze travelling over his long, lean length, and trying not to see the reckless gleam in his deep-set eyes that was probably connected to the bottle of wine he held.

She didn't remember him ever drinking much.

'Don't worry, I'm not drunk, at least not yet.'

The words sounded almost like a threat. Their glances connected and the combustible quality of his dark gleaming stare made her stomach tighten and flutter.

His glance took in her damp hair, which was drying into a nimbus of fiery curls, before his eyes narrowed in again on her face. 'Were you avoiding me?'

Her attempt at laughing off the suggestion sounded pretty feeble even to her own ears. 'I could ask you the same question,' she tossed back. Only she wouldn't because that would have been absurd.

'I should have gone tonight,' he admitted.

She glanced at the bottle in his hand and arched a brow. 'Celebrating?'

'That remains to be seen.'

She refused to be ruffled or think about the hidden meaning in his words... Actually, was it so hidden? She suddenly felt queasy at the image of a warm body ready and waiting for him in bed.

'Spare me the details.'

He laughed. 'I have always thought the joy was in the detail.'

Jane, who had spent the last four years trying very hard not to remember the joy or the detail of Draco's lovemaking, cleared her throat. 'You still haven't said why you didn't go tonight.'

'I don't remember you being so... Actually, tonight is mostly experts, great people but they can be a bit... intense. There will be a more diverse group arriving to-morrow, more relaxed.'

A nasty thought was forming in her head. Was this all about revenge? Was she here so that he could see her humiliated, exposing her ignorance when she found herself among experts? A moment later she felt guilty for the thought. She had done enough online research to know that Draco's green credentials were not some marketing ploy, that he appeared to have a genuine pas-sion and if he had wanted to see her make a fool of her-self he would have been there to watch.

'I'm not an expert,' she pointed out spikily, deter-mined not to fall back into old patterns of behaviour. Her compliant silences were long gone.

'No, you're not.' Except in the field of driving him slightly crazy. What was it about her? He watched through dark hooded eyes as her hand went to the base of her throat and he remembered kissing the blue-veined pulse point.

His desire for her had never made any logical sense. It had always been consuming, and he had always vowed not to be consumed by a woman.

'Did you want me to make a fool of myself tonight?'

The charge dragged him from his contemplation of the sliver of midriff where the pale skin glowed with an opalescent sheen against the vivid brightness of her shirt.

'Why would I want that?' he asked slowly.

'Maybe a bit of payback…?'

'A boring evening and finding yourself out of your depth hardly compares with being left standing at the altar.'

The guilty heat flew to her cheeks and her antagonism melted into remorse—not that she regretted her decision; she knew it had been the right one, but she wished that she had made it earlier.

'I'm sorry.'

'Sorry?' He considered the word. 'Oh, that makes it all right, then,' he drawled. 'Did you save the article with my face attached on coercive control?'

'What?' Her eyes flew wide with horror. 'But that's not true! And your press release.' Not that it had been his—mysterious sources had managed to subtly distance Draco from the entire event. The story was then buried by a convenient good news story—who doesn't love a royal baby?

'When did the truth get in the way of a good story or, in that particular instance, innuendo?' he said, sounding to her ears astonishingly casual about the whole thing. 'The mutual agreement story was not universally accepted. I suppose I should consider myself lucky no one asked you to contribute to the debate.'

'No one found me and I would never have called you a bully!' she exclaimed indignantly.

'You did earlier.'

She conceded the point with an uncomfortable shrug. 'Well, that was different. I nearly ran you over. I was… you were…'

He arched a brow.

'Impossible!' she burst out. 'I know you are rather overbearing and you treat women with the sort of respect you show your suits, but you are not a bully, no way, and—'

His slow whistle cut across her. 'I really know where to go for a character reference should I need one!'

'Nobody ever found me, but if they had I would not have contributed to a character assassination!' she exclaimed indignantly. 'And you were not at fault, I was, and I never meant to hurt you, Draco, truly I didn't, but it was the right thing, you know that, outside the bedroom,' she said, immediately wishing she hadn't voiced the thought, or at least the bedroom part, because his eyes darkened instantly and the tension in the air made the fine hairs on her nape lift.

'We didn't have a thing in common.'

'Outside the bedroom,' he inserted provocatively.

'That doesn't last. We would have split up by now.'

'I lack your ability to see into the future, especially a future that never happened.'

She sighed out her frustration. This was going around in circles. 'Look I don't see any point in post-mortems. You are angry, I behaved badly, and you deserved an apology, more than just a note.'

'A note!' He shook his dark head. 'There was no note.'

Jane began to rub her bare finger. 'I put it in with the ring—you got the ring?' The idea that the valuable item had gone astray filled her with horror, as did the idea he might think she had kept it, or sold it.

He nodded. 'I read the delivery note. I was aware of the parcel but I did not open it.'

'Oh, right… Well, I wrote a note to say that I was sorry.'

'It was a long time ago. There is no need for an orgy of remorse. We have both moved on.'

She lowered her eyes and nodded. 'I know.'

'And you found another life too? How long did you know the father…?'

'Robert. Not that long.'

His expression hardened at her deliberate vagueness. 'So he was not waiting in the wings to comfort you when our marriage didn't happen?'

For a split second she took the question at face value, remembering how she had felt after she had run away from their wedding.

Then his underlying meaning hit her.

'There was no one else involved in my decision to—'

'Dump me at the altar.'

She winced but then brought her chin up. 'How could you think that?'

He gave a negligent shrug. 'Just a passing thought.' One that had been torturing him since the moment he had learnt of the child's existence. 'Does he walk yet? The child?'

'Mattie.'

'Yes, Mattie.'

'No, he's too young, but according to the books that's when life really changes.'

'Will your cottage be suitable then?'

Her chin went up. 'The cottage is perfect!' she declared with a dangerous sparkle in her eyes. 'I wouldn't want to live anywhere else even if I could afford it.'

'You struggle?'

'We do fine. The house belonged to Robert's great-aunt.' And it was now Mattie's inheritance.

The small amount she could save might not be enough to enable her to buy a place of her own, but she'd be happy with a rental when Mattie turned eighteen, maybe staying near the village.

'So there is no mortgage or rent.' There were plenty of other bills though. 'I should be getting back to Mattie. Val seems lovely and very competent, but I only came down for a few minutes to grab a bite…'

His eyes went to her hand, which retained the squashed remains of a sandwich. 'Literally, it would seem,' he murmured, before adding in a tone of clipped annoyance, 'Why were you not offered the option of a meal in your room?'

Because he had delivered the question in a 'heads will roll' sort of way, she added quickly, 'I was, everyone here has been super kind, but I wasn't that hungry and I wanted to get my bearings.'

'You should eat.'

His accusing tone made her blink, then frown at the underlying impatience. 'I have eaten.' She gave a small smile of triumph and swallowed the squashed bit of sandwich to illustrate her point.

'A sandwich,' he said with lip-curling contempt. 'It is no wonder you are so...' Draco paused, his eyelids half lowering as his glance skimmed her body. He was prepared for the primal reaction of his body, but not the surge of protectiveness. She looked so small, so delicate, so vulnerable.

Jane raised a brow and allowed the awkward silence to stretch. It was a bit late for him to worry about being polite. That ship had sailed the moment he'd opened his mouth to call her skinny, bony or whatever other unflattering adjectives were going through his mind.

'Not the woman you proposed to in another life?' He was probably thinking he'd had a lucky escape. 'And you're right, actually—I am not that woman. And you have no idea what a relief it is not to have to play that role!'

'So you were playing a role when we made love, playing a role when you couldn't keep your greedy little hands off me, *cara*,' he drawled. 'You are a very good actress.

'I meant meek and submissive—'

'Except in bed—' He had never had such a fierce

lover in his life, or one so sensitive to his needs, and not afraid to tell him what hers were.

She lifted her hands above her head and turned her back on him. 'Will you stop talking about—?'

'Talking about what? Sex? You have changed. I seem to recall it was your favourite subject.'

Her eyes narrowed and her chin-tilted pugnacity made him think of a small, cute dog that thought it was large and dangerous—not that she yapped, even when angry. He'd always liked her voice, the softness underlaid with a sexy hint of huskiness that grew more pronounced when she was aroused.

'I lied. I wanted to bag a billionaire!'

A heavy silence followed her words. 'Clearly not enough.'

Jane shed her antagonism like a second skin. She knew how it must have hurt a proud man like Draco to be left at the altar. 'I hadn't met Rob…anyone,' she said, still genuinely bewildered by that accusation. 'Why would you say that?'

'You have a child, you have lost weight, you look like a shadow, you are grieving…' he ground out. 'This much is obvious. It is obvious to your community, which is clearly protective of you. Are you trying to tell me this man had nothing to do with why you dumped me so publicly?' He bit down hard on further emotional incoherent revelations escaping his clamped lips.

Bit late, Draco, mocked the ironic voice in his head.

You can't have it both ways, he thought. Tell yourself you had a lucky escape and you have moved on—

he had so many meaningless notches in his bedpost to prove it—and then come across as some sort of victim, unable to move on.

Jane was so astonished by his uncharacteristic outburst that it took her several moments to follow through the processes that had brought him to this conclusion.

Here it was again, another opportunity, red lights flashing, to set the record straight, to correct the facts, to admit she was not a mother.

That she had never loved anyone but him.

She knew that she was a coward, she despised herself for taking shelter in a misconception, but where was the harm? she asked her guilty conscience.

She'd hurt him and he'd survived. At least this way she got to keep her secret, hug it to herself and know she had done the right thing. She deserved some privacy. This was her own private tragedy.

She laughed, and she didn't know why, and saw his face darken.

He looked as if he wanted to throttle her and actually she couldn't blame him. Then she thought about the stream of beautiful women who he had had sex with… Good Lord, she had been on the brink of feeling sorry for him. How insane was that?

'I should have done it privately,' she admitted. 'And for that I apologise.'

'But you don't regret it.'

Calmness settled over her as she saw babies with dark hair and beautiful dark eyes. 'Not for one second. We

had great sex, Draco, but to spend a lifetime together...
you know what a bad fit I was.'

The irony was he had, and it hadn't mattered. His desire for her, the elemental fire she lit in his blood, had bypassed logic.

'I... I have to get back to Mattie,' she said, desperate to escape before she cried. She turned and ran back towards the lights.

CHAPTER EIGHT

'SORRY I WAS so long.'

The young woman uncurled her legs and stood up from the sofa she had been ensconced in. 'You weren't, and Mattie has not made a sound. He is fast asleep. You have eaten? You didn't get lost?'

Jane struggled to smile back. 'Your directions were excellent.' It was her instincts that were not at all excellent. Her instincts were all wrong. 'I think I will just make myself a tea and go to bed,' she said, feigning a realistic yawn.

An hour and two teas later her yawn was real, but her mind was still painfully active.

This had been a massive mistake. The only question was should she cut her losses now or see it out to the grim end?

She changed into a nightdress and looked at the bed but didn't climb in. The idea of lying there tossing and turning was not a tempting proposition. Instead she did another tour of the nursery suite, looking inside the playroom for the first time.

It really was magical, she decided as she opened one of the cupboards at the end to reveal floor-to-ceiling shelves stacked with games and toys. Wandering over to the twin cupboard beside it, she noticed this one had a key. She turned it and these doors folded back to reveal, not shelves of toys, but a bathroom twice the size of the one she'd used earlier with twin sinks, a massive copper bath and a shower cubicle still emitting a cloud of steam into the atmosphere.

She wasn't looking at the impressive fitments but at the man who was standing stark naked and wet in the middle of the room.

Draco, his face hawkish, the skin drawn tight against the perfect bones, returned her stare with one that glittered with bold challenge. A small, dangerous smile played around his sensual lips, his dark olive skin gleaming gold, the moisture clinging to the dusting of body hair, his long eyelashes.

Her eyes dropped. She couldn't help herself—he was so beautiful, like a statue brought to warm, vibrant life. There was not an ounce of excess flesh on his lean frame to hide the perfect definition of each muscle.

Her heart thudding, her helpless glance slid down his chest, his corrugated ribbed belly and lower. Her breath caught and snagged in her chest as she struggled to breathe. Draco had always represented the epitome of raw masculine power and he was aroused.

Very aroused.

She tried to kick-start her brain and managed a stuttered, 'S-sorry.' She took a step back, only it wasn't. The signals had got crossed in her head and she took a step forward, drawn towards all that magnetic potency.

'I'm sorry, I had no idea that the door…'

He dropped the towel in his hand and turned to fully face her, totally at ease with his naked state. 'It was locked on your side. You opened it, *tesoro*.'

'I didn't know…this is…' She stopped and thought, Why aren't I closing it?

'Because you don't want to?'

She swallowed. 'I said that out loud? 'This is…'

'Come here, Jane.'

She shook her head. 'I won't… I can't. This is a massive mistake.'

He swore. 'We are very good at making massive mistakes together, I think,' he returned sardonically. 'We both know we would have ended up here.'

She shook her head in helpless denial and ran her tongue across her dry lips. If he touched her she'd be lost to all sense and all sanity.

So instead she touched him.

She laid a hand against his chest, feeling his damp warm skin under her splayed fingers and holding his eyes.

She watched his eyes blacken, saw the muscle beside his clenched jaw tighten and felt the pulse of excitement between her thighs. Desire was a thudding presence in her head.

He bent down, his breath on her face as he slid a slow kiss across her lips, a butterfly kiss that left her wanting more. Draco always left her wanting more.

She took his hand and guided it to her breast, then some tiny flicker of sanity pierced the sensual thrall she was on the brink of surrendering to and she shook her head.

'Mattie?'

'Leave the door open and—' He reached out to a shelf and located a control pad. Pressing a button, he raised his hands. 'It activates the intercom in here too.'

'You can listen to me?'

'I love listening to you when you make those little mewling noises in your throat, that little...' He swallowed and reached out, whipping the nightdress off in one smooth action. It fell on the damp floor in a crumpled heap.

She felt relief and then, when his stare slid lower, a moment of panic. She was too thin, she was—

'Beautiful!'

The throaty declaration made her confidence surge and her own gaze lift.

As they met flesh to flesh, kissing wildly, sparks struck and flamed. Jane plastered herself against him, her small breasts flattened against his chest as she lifted herself on her toes. And when his hands came to span her waist and her toes left the floor she wound her legs around his waist as he carried her into the next room.

A bedroom—the only detail she noted was the big bed.

He laid her in it and knelt beside her as he lowered her head, admitting with a wicked grin, 'I didn't think I'd make it this far.'

'I love touching you,' she husked as her greedy hands explored the hard contours of his chest, his back. She pressed her lips to his chest, only stopping when he tangled his fingers in her hair and pushed her head down onto the bed.

She whispered his name as he kissed her, his hands moving over her body leaving trails of fire and screaming nerve endings. Her fingers slid into his dark hair, holding his face at her breasts as she writhed beneath the caress of his tongue and mouth.

He lifted his head. 'You look like an angel, the wanton wild variety.'

She moaned and bit down on her lips as he slid his hand between her legs, his finger slipping into the hot moisture of her body.

He only stopped when her finger slid across the velvet hardness of his tip, her hand closing as she tightened her grip around his shaft. Wriggling beneath him, she reversed their positions and moved down his body, tracking a line on his damp skin with her tongue.

A wild animal groan was torn from the vault of his chest as he dragged her up his body until their faces were level, his hands cupping her bottom.

The raw need etched in his face was beyond exciting.

'You taste of me,' he slurred against her mouth as they kissed. 'I need...'

She saw what he was about to do and said quickly, 'No, it's okay, I'm not... I have it covered.'

A strange expression flickered across his face but a moment later it was gone and he nodded. 'I'm safe too. Tested. And when I am inside you there is no one else.'

She could have wept. There had only ever been him. Did he really think she could think of anyone else? 'I need you inside me,' she whispered, sliding her tongue along his lips and then inside his mouth.

As his control broke he tipped her onto her back.

'I have to have you now.'

She silently nodded and strained up towards him as he slid a knee between her thighs, nudging the aching moisture between her legs. She pushed against him to ease the ache, the need.

Then as he slid into her in one thrust she yelled his name, her fingernails digging into his back for purchase.

'You're like silk,' he groaned against her neck and the pulse inside her built and built until they were both on fire.

Then she hit the peak and shuddered, feeling the heat spill deep into her.

'What are you doing?' A heavy arm was flung across her. 'What time…?'

She pressed a finger to his lips and wriggled sinuously from under his arm.

'I have to go.'

He sat up, looking gorgeously rumpled but suddenly very awake.

'It's the rule.'

'Whose rule?'

She ignored the appeal of his white devilish grin, along with the lazy, slumbrous invitation in his eyes as he lay there, his hands tucked behind his head, in a pose that said, I'm yours…come and get me.

She wanted to but this needed saying.

'Mine. Look, if this is going to happen again it will be on my terms.'

His eyes narrowed speculatively as he raised himself on one elbow to look at her. 'Is this because you feel guilty, disloyal that we had sex?'

It would have hurt less if he'd said made love.

There had never been any pretence of love, yet there had been tender moments. A touch, a look that had had the power to bring tears to her eyes, a reaction countered by the longing to hear him voice the feelings that she now knew had been nothing but a product of her own wishful thinking.

She would not make that mistake again. She would accept the reality and enjoy it while it lasted.

She lifted her chin. 'I am not the woman I was… I won't…'

'Say what you imagined I want to hear… Yes, I get that,' he said sardonically. 'And it is why… I like that idea. I like the idea of sex as equals, no emotional barriers. You are grieving, but we still have needs… Sex is a natural human urge, and I think a lot—I think a lot of being inside you,' he admitted throatily, allowing himself to admit that his desire for her was utterly insatiable.

That had not changed, but his sense of self-preservation made him refuse to acknowledge that her vulnerability hurt him—he always had considered empathy something to avoid.

Nothing that had happened had made him change his mind, except that ship had sailed. He couldn't even pretend an indifference to her feelings.

The silence pulsated.

'Is this why you connived, and if you deny it I won't believe you, you connived, pulled strings and, well, the stuff you do in your sleep, Draco, to have me here in your bed?'

'I did not have to drag you here, *cara*.'

'No, but—' She took a deep breath, planting both fists against her chest as she pushed out, 'There are rules. Don't look like that. This is not a joke to me,' she flared.

'All right, what are your rules?'

Her lips tightened at the suggestion he was humouring her. 'Well, for starters, this stays private.'

'I was not about to invite an audience.'

Jane slung him a look, annoyed that he didn't seem to be taking this seriously. 'You know what I mean, no public displays of...'

'Affection?' he inserted when she stumbled searching for the right word.

She refused to let his sarcastic interruption put her off. 'This is sex, not commitment.' She almost felt stupid pointing this out, but the rule was for her own benefit as much as his. The best way to avoid heartache was by killing dead any irrational expectations before they took root. 'And most importantly you need to understand that, for me, Mattie always comes first.'

The silence that had grown heavier as she spoke stretched.

Draco was not questioning her words, but his own reaction to them, which ought to have been living the dream...? Sex with no expectations of it becoming something else, no romantic gestures or pretending to feel what he didn't.

He was not normally on the receiving end of rules, which might account for the irrational surge of dissatisfaction underlying his response.

'It sounds workable,' he finally responded coolly.

There was nothing cool about the smouldering expression in his eyes as he dragged her down to lie on top of him.

Every cell in her body wanted to relax into him, meld her curves to his hard frame, but one cell of sanity enabled her to draw back. She just prayed he would never know how hard it was for her to roll away. He made no attempt to prevent her.

'I need to get back to Mattie.'

'I will be away tomorrow,' he heard himself say in some sort of reflexive response to the rejection.

Fine.

With her hand halfway to Mattie's mouth with a spoonful of baby gunge Jane was telling him was super-delicious, her own mouth fell open.

She might even be drooling.

'I thought you were away today?'

Her accusatory tone was aligned with the fact that Draco was not away. He was here, radiating an electrical charge of energy that sent her nervous system into shameful overload.

'You decided to eat in the nursery,' he said, not addressing her comment or his presence. He surveyed the table. 'Except you are not eating.'

'I have had coffee and some fruit.' She blinked as someone in uniform appeared with a trolley bearing waffles and scrambled eggs. At least those were the items she could identify.

'I didn't order these.'

'No, I did. You sit and eat. I will feed the baby.'

'You...?'

He arched a brow. 'You think me incapable of managing this task?' he challenged, wondering if she might be right.

Jane, who would have actually paid to see him manage this task, put the spoon down and, lips twitching, stepped away. 'Feel free.'

'When you sit down and eat.' He pulled out one of the chairs beside the open window and gestured.

After a gentle push she took the seat and, actually, the smell wafting up from the bowl of fluffy scrambled eggs was not unpleasant.

She had eaten a plateful and two slices of toast dripping with butter when she broke down, laughing, as the expression of fierce determination on Draco's face vanished when a lump of mashed baby food landed in his eye.

He pulled out a spare chair and straddled it, wiping his face with a napkin. 'I think he has finished.'

'All it took to bring a sex god down to earth was an eight-month-old baby. Who knew?' she mocked, grinning.

'A sex god…you think?' he mused, sliding her a self-satisfied look that made her oversensitive stomach flip as he poured himself some coffee. 'There are limits to my willingness to become an object of mockery. I have fed him. You can remove the food that did not land in his mouth.'

'You gave him the spoon.'

'Good for developing his dexterity and self-reliance,' he came back glibly.

'Seriously, Draco, I thought you were—'

'My plans changed,' he cut in, not quite meeting her eyes. 'So I decided to check on you. Does that break any of your rules?' He found himself really beginning to resent those rules.

'I don't think... No, probably not.'

'I normally begin my day with a swim. Would you care to join me?'

'Mattie—'

'It is my understanding that it is never too soon to introduce a baby to water, and if you are worried about exposing his delicate skin to the sun we have an indoor complex as well as the outdoor pools.'

'Of course you do,' she came back drily. 'Oh, why not? That would be nice, but he might not like it,' she warned.

Draco had managed fifteen minutes of laps, pushing his body to the physical limits, before Jane appeared, and his body reacted independently of his brain to the sight of her standing there in a plain black relatively modest swimsuit, revealing that he had not reached his physical limits at all.

Actually it turned out that, after a first startled, wide-eyed look, Mattie did like the water. So did Jane but who wouldn't?

The indoor pool was Roman themed, decorated from floor to ceiling with mosaic tiles of varying shades of blue all set against a background of gold, which gave a shimmering, breathtaking effect. The murals on the walls were classically inspired.

'You want to swim? I could take him?'

'You want to take Mattie?'

Want, Draco privately conceded, would have been overstating it.

'Any instructions? Keep his head out of the water, is that right?' he teased.

Jane handed him over with an eye roll, trying not to lust too obviously over Draco's streamlined muscular frame and failing dramatically as she handed the baby over to his care, without, despite her reluctance, a qualm.

She always felt safe, at least physically, with Draco and she totally trusted him with Mattie.

She had managed a few lazy lengths of the middle pool—there were three—when she flipped onto her back, floating as she watched Draco, in the shallowest pool, swirl Mattie around before splashing him gently, resulting in the baby's loud gurgling chuckle echoing off the ceiling.

An expression of sadness slid across her face and her heart tightened as she thought of the things that would never be.

One day Draco would make an incredible father.

Despite her belief in his fathering qualities, Draco was not involved in the soothing of the fretful baby post swim or the changing, feeding and settling.

Jane joined him again, very conscious of the heavy achy feeling low in her pelvis, aware as she lowered herself into the warmer shallower pool that his eyes were watching her every move.

'I need to make some calls.'

She nodded and told herself the bubble of disappointment was irrational. She had made the rules after all.

'Enjoy your day,' he said, levering himself from the pool.

Jane averted her eyes from the tall dripping figure as he slicked back his dark hair. 'We will,' she promised.

'You have plans?'

'I'm playing it by ear.'

It was mid-afternoon when the prickle on the back of her neck alerted her to the fact she was no longer alone.

'He's asleep?'

Without turning, Jane put a finger to her lips and tiptoed out of the room, aware that Draco had followed her. She felt his hand on her shoulder and found herself leaning back against him.

'Is this,' he began, the throaty rasp of his voice against her ear sending electric shudders through her body, 'when I am allowed *my* moment?'

With a deep sigh, her green eyes glowing with slumbrous invitation, she turned in the circle of his arms, straining up to brush her lips against his. 'You are allowed anything and everything,' she husked, her lips moving across his mouth before she slid her tongue between his lips, pushing away the thought that there was a time limit on this bliss. These moments were too few, too precious—she wouldn't allow anything to spoil them.

Her fellow attendees seemed an eclectic bunch and during the introductory talk several came over to say hello to Mattie. At the coffee break Jane sat at an empty table and positioned Mattie's buggy at her side, catching the toy he threw before it hit the floor. She gave it back to him and turned back to her coffee and the screen of her phone, scrolling through the bewildering list of classes on offer, glancing up when a young couple approached.

'Mind if we join you?'

Jane smiled.

'I'm Luciana, this is Joe.' Before Jane could respond she added, 'And we know this is Mattie, he really is a star, and you are...'

'Jane.'

'You made your choices on classes yet?' Luciana asked, casting a knowledgeable eye at the screen of Jane's phone.

'So far I haven't even figured out what most of them are... I really think I might be out of my depth,' she admitted ruefully. 'What does NZSD stand for?'

It was the young man who responded. 'Net zero and sustainability development.' He saw Jane's surprised expression and grinned. 'I know I look Latin but I'm Liverpool through and through. When in doubt I use the "close your eyes and stick a pin in" methodology. Or, better still, get engaged to a local like I did and let her decide for me.'

'Are you calling me bossy?' Luciana retorted, extending her hand to show the sparkling ring on her finger.

Jane made the appropriate admiring noises.

'So you are staying in the palazzo?'

Jane nodded and wondered if that was her role for the next three weeks.

The woman staying in the palazzo.

'I think the idea is Mattie doesn't keep people awake at night.'

* * *

Into the second week of the course, on what had been scheduled as a free day Jane sat down to breakfast. When, for the first time, Draco did not appear to share breakfast with her and Mattie, she realised that without intending to they had settled into a kind of routine.

Recognising that his no-show left her feeling a sense of something approaching loss, Jane realised that her rules were not a guaranteed method of protecting her heart from damage.

'Rules aren't much use if you don't follow them, are they, Mattie?' she told her uncritical audience as she popped him in his stroller, struggling to retain her cheery attitude when she realised that very soon there would be no breakfasts and no anything else with Draco.

She took Mattie for an early morning swim alone, determined that she would enjoy the day, which she had not planned to spend with Draco anyway. She had signed up for the trip to the local town.

It would be more relaxing without Draco around, she told herself. Their shared sexual awareness could make even the most mundane action breathtakingly intimate and made it hard to remember the rules were there for a reason, let alone what they were.

CHAPTER NINE

DRACO APPEARED LATER that day just as she was settling Mattie for his afternoon nap, or trying to.

'Did you enjoy your morning?'

'Very much. It was good to get away.' And the local town, with its historic cobbled streets and harbour, was really beautiful.

'Good to get away from me?'

Soon every day would be away from Draco. She felt her stomach tighten and pushed away the thought, painting on a smile as she surreptitiously studied his face, observing that the same indefinable thing she had heard in his voice echoed in his lean features.

Had he got out of the wrong side of the bed?

It had not been hers.

When Mattie had kicked off she had wheeled his crib to beside her bed. Draco had been lying there, the sheet low over his hips to reveal the light dusting of dark hair on his flat, muscle-ridged belly and broad bronzed chest, one hand behind his head, looking gloriously tousled and, with the stubble on his jaw, even more mind-numbingly sexy than normal as he'd watched her.

He hadn't said a thing.

He hadn't needed to. Having caught a glimpse of herself in the mirror, Jane could imagine what he'd been thinking! Her hair a wild mess of curls, dark shadows under her eyes and her hip bones visible through the thin robe she had quickly pulled on.

She had tried to sound as if she didn't care when she had suggested in a scratchy, impatient voice that if he wanted any sleep he should make the trip through the interconnecting door to his own bedroom suite. Would he make the same trip when his own children were here, or would the nanny be in the nursery while Draco made love to his perfect wife?

Later, when Mattie had settled and she had rolled over to sleep, missing the warm body beside her, she had regretted her generosity.

She ignored the lingering sick feeling in the pit of her stomach and managed to respond to his question with a teasing smile and a negligent shrug. 'Oh, absolutely, you weren't there to cramp my style.'

'You did the usual tourist stuff. You ate?' he added.

'Well, I am pretty much a tourist,' she pointed out. 'And of course I ate. I know you think I'm too skinny, but I do not have to be force-fed.'

'You are not too skinny! You are—' Tough and vulnerable, and the combination shook loose some uncomfortable emotions in him that he was not prepared to own. 'I like watching you eat. When you remember, you eat like you make love—with total commitment.'

The frown melted from her face. 'Yes, well, I love the local cuisine and it's quite nice not to have to cook. I'm a terrible cook,' she confided with a rueful grin. 'Actually Luciana showed me a few places only the locals would know about.' She glanced at the dress, hanging up behind the door, she had found in the incredible vintage shop down a side alley. It had been an Aladdin's cave, a treasure trove of vintage and rare, owned by an equally fascinating woman.

In her mind's eye Jane could see the dress as it would be shortly. Her fingers itched to get to work on it.

'You didn't have to go on the minibus. I would have taken you and Mattie if you'd asked,' Draco observed, continuing to sound disgruntled.

'Mattie was fine. He's a very sociable baby.' Though not, admittedly, today. He was not his usual cheery self. 'And you weren't there,' she said, keeping her tone neutral, then adding brightly before he responded, 'It was actually nice to be part of the group and not the woman who is staying at the palazzo.'

'Has that been an issue?'

She shrugged. 'People are initially wary of the person being given preferential treatment, but Mattie is always a vote winner.' And everyone could see that it made sense they had been given more baby-friendly rooms.

Of course, if they had realised that she was sleeping with Draco she could imagine that situation would change very quickly! Which was a very good reason, one among many, to stick to the rules and keep the sleeping arrangement under the radar. It was important to her for people to know she was here on her own merits, which she liked to think she was, or at least deserved to be.

There were some fascinating characters, and she

was learning a lot, some of which would be transfer-
able when she got back home.

Some days…home seemed a very long way away, in
another life, but she had to keep her feet on the ground
and remember the life she was living now was not real.
A week and a half and she would be back home.

'Everyone is very excited about the party tonight.'

He raised a sceptical brow as he looked at her with
narrowed eyes. 'Everyone?'

She shrugged. The truth was, when Draco had said
that there was to be a cocktail party to celebrate the
first of what he intended would be a yearly course and
conference and he was inviting some people, she had
been concerned that someone there might have been at
the wedding and might recognise her. She didn't want
to be outed as the runaway bride!

'I'm not really a party person, but yes, I'm sure it
will be…interesting. Will there be many of your friends
there?' To her dismay she did not pull off the casual part
of her question.

'Just spit it out, *cara*.'

'I was worrying that…' The words came in a rush.
'Will there be people there who were at the…wedding?'

'You think they will recognise you? You were hardly
there long enough for that.'

The acid sarcasm brought a flush to her pale cheeks.
She touched her red hair, which today she had loosely
gathered in a knot from which bronzed curls spilled out
and framed her face.

'People see the hair.'

'Indeed they do,' he agreed as he thought of the texture, how it looked spread out on the pillow catching the sun and burning burnished gold when she lay sleeping in the morning.

'There is no need to be concerned. It is a different set of guests, diverse, but all people whose attendance will raise the profile of the event and hopefully more to follow. Also I am announcing the launch of a prize for an eco-initiative for young people. These guests are contacts that will be useful. It is not black tie tonight, but I can have a selection of outfits—'

Exasperated, she cut across him. 'We have already had this discussion, Draco, and I'm not wearing jeans and a nice top, if that is what you're worried about.' Actually Luciana, the willowy Italian girl, had offered her a dress that, though mini on its owner, would have been mid-calf on Jane, but with the waist cinched in would have done nicely. She had found a suitable belt but then found the rather nicer alternative.

'I think you look delightful in jeans.' He quite enjoyed peeling them down her slim legs. The top was to his mind nice or otherwise optional.

'I have my outfit sorted. I found something in town this morning.'

He looked dubious. 'There are not many shops in—'

She gave a small smile and sighed at his persistence. 'You mean designer shops and no, there aren't, but there are a few really good small independent stores and I discovered an absolutely incredible vintage shop. The flamboyant elderly lady who owned it had many tales to tell of her time working in the film industry.'

At one point she had brought out an album of signed

photos of old film stars, pleased to find an audience that was genuinely fascinated.

Jane had come away with the blue silk thirties dress in really great condition, which was now hanging behind her door, and the promise that the next time she came there would be cakes.

Jane had assured her that cakes would be much appreciated, feeling sad when she'd realised that she wouldn't be here for a return visit.

The dress needed a few tweaks but nothing that was beyond her capabilities. Would that her life could be sorted so painlessly—a snip here, a stitch there.

'I don't think she does it for the money. I think she just loves beautiful things.'

'You bought a second-hand dress?' He sounded so comically shocked at the idea that she smiled as she gestured to the dress.

'I did.'

'You are wearing that?'

'How lucky I don't need your approval to feel good about myself,' she tossed back. 'It was a bargain. I felt quite guilty.'

Seeing the antagonistic challenge in the eyes turned to him, Draco swallowed the protest on his lips. Obviously she would look gorgeous in anything, but she deserved to wear beautiful clothes and not someone's hand-me-downs.

'So what time would you like to walk across?'

She raised a feathery brow. 'To the party? Oh, I'll make my own way across.'

She saw his jaw clamp but he didn't say a word as

he pushed his hands into his pockets and turned to the window. She sighed. Draco's back was very expressive.

She finished folding the last of the baby sleep suits, extracted a grumbling Mattie from his stroller and, performing a soothing jiggle to quieten the baby, walked across to where Draco stood, a tower of glowering disapproval.

'I don't know why you are being so cranky.'

He spun around to face her. 'Cranky?' he echoed, sounding so incredulous at the suggestion that she almost laughed, but stopped herself, realising that might be unnecessarily provocative.

She glanced down at the baby in her arms, whose eyes had drifted closed, but, to be on the safe side, didn't stop rocking him. 'Well, it is sometimes difficult to work out who the baby in the room is.'

His expression of utter outraged astonishment drew a short laugh from her throat…before she held her breath, waiting for him to explode. She released it again when he laughed, reluctantly, but Jane decided she'd take it.

'Well, it is daft, isn't it?' she observed with a smile. 'It's not as if it's a date. We have established that we don't do dates.'

She watched with a sinking feeling in the pit of her stomach as his expression changed, the humour wiped out to be replaced by a dark scowl.

'So you wish to leave your options open. If you go alone you can leave with who you wish.'

His interpretation immediately fired Jane up. She was spending all her time and energy trying to maintain the boundaries and keep to the rules and Draco seemed not even to recognise they were there! If they came down she would have to see that all those self-imposed lines were not just invisible, they were utterly useless. She didn't want her delusions to be revealed, because then she would have to admit she was not in control of this situation. She was not in control of anything. Her emotions didn't recognise any lines, invisible or otherwise, and at some point this was going to hurt.

All over again!

'That's a crazy, not to mention insulting, suggestion!' she retorted, her voice shaking as she clung to her control by her fingernails. 'Be careful, Draco, or I might walk away with the idea you are jealous,' she threw out in frustration, not expecting her words to find a mark.

The words stopped Draco cold.

An image flashed into his head, his father consumed with jealousy demanding that his wife, her bags packed, tell him who the man was she was leaving him for. And she had laughed contemptuously at him, falling to his knees begging her to stay, degrading himself, literally crawling after her.

He stood there trying to shift his brain into gear, the pressure in his chest heavy.

'I am sorry to disappoint you but I do not do jealousy,' he said finally.

She saw his closed expression and asked herself what else she had expected. 'I am aware.'

He looked at her through narrowed eyes. 'Do you still feel guilty for having sex with me so soon after your partner's death? Is that what this is about?'

'I have no idea what the "this" you are talking about

is,' she replied, guilt putting an acidic note in her voice. 'And I resent being looked at like I'm a bug under a microscope...a...psychological experiment.' And a liar. She felt several kinds of terrible for taking refuge in a lie that just seemed to grow and grow the longer she hadn't addressed it.

Now it was too late.

'Which is why you can't meet my eyes?'

She met his eyes then, her green eyes sparking fire, and directed a defiant look at him. 'This is not something I want to discuss with you. People do not— I don't feel guilty, Draco. I feel—' She paused and thought, I feel scared stiff, because the illusion that I can have sex and not fall in love with you is making me feel ill, especially as I never fell out.

For a split second she wondered what he'd do if she voiced the words out loud. He might really think he wanted to know what her motivations were, mainly because he couldn't believe that any woman would say no to him. But he would regret it if I did, she thought grimly.

'So you will have sex with me, but you won't walk a few hundred metres and enter a cocktail party beside me.'

'I suppose that about covers it,' she said, noting her deliberately cheery delivery was making him look even more bad-tempered, in a way that beautiful people and sleek jungle cats looked bad-tempered. 'And will you lower your voice? Mattie is just settling. He has been a bit cranky today.'

Draco watched her look down at the baby in her arms,

concern pleating her brow, and something shifted in his chest. It was happening a lot.

She was, he had to admit, a perfect mother.

Some masochistic impulse made him throw salt in the open wound as his inner voice said, A mother, but not of your babies.

Fine by him. He didn't want babies.

When had he decided that he would leave the passing of their dubious genes to his little brother?

Could that change of heart have anything to do with the only woman he had ever imagined being the mother of his children leaving him standing at the altar?

Ignoring the taunting voice in his head, he ground out a frustrated, 'This is absurd.'

'What is absurd?'

'You are being absurd. Are you trying to make some sort of point?'

The moment he flung the words it hit Draco that he could just as easily ask himself the same question.

Why was he getting so hung up on this? It wasn't as if he *wanted* a relationship. Or was it that *she* very obviously didn't that was getting to him?

Was he arguing with her or his own responses?

Turning her head to deliver an exasperated glare, Jane caught an indecipherable expression on Draco's face, but by the time she had laid the drowsy baby in his buggy it had gone.

Draco watched as she dropped into a chair before hooking one small foot onto the metal rest intended for a bag and on auto pilot began to push it back and forth with a metronome regularity meant to soothe the baby to sleep.

She looked exhausted.

Emotions he kept a tight hold of threatened to break loose in his chest as he studied her face, the shadows under her green eyes, the pallor that made the sprinkling of freckles stand out across her nose and cheeks.

She had looked exhausted last night when she had brought the baby back to bed and kicked him out, so much so that he had heard himself offer to take the baby for a drive. He had heard it said—where, he couldn't remember—that this was helpful for some crying babies.

She had looked at him really oddly and said thanks, but no, thanks, she…they were fine, as if she was drawing a firm line around an inner circle he would never be allowed inside.

Not that he wanted to be, obviously.

'Yes.'

He shook his head.

'Yes, I am trying to make a point. I am going to this cocktail party on my own, not as some sort of arm-candy accessory. Nobody will ever treat me seriously if they think I am your latest girlfriend.'

She made it sound as if it were the worst fate in the world! Controlling his slug of anger and the impulse to respond with a childish retort along the lines of she should be so lucky, which would have made him sound like the total loser she appeared to think he was, he rose to his feet, the abrupt action making the baby stir in his sleep, which earned him a reproachful look from under her lashes.

It was bizarre, almost as if he had walked into an alternative reality. He spent his days sidestepping the women who threw themselves at him, never hearing no if he chose to assuage his physical needs, and here was Jane keeping him at arm's length.

Arm's length was generally where he wanted to be, so the situation should have pleased him.

He dragged both hands through his hair and stalked across to the window before turning back.

'So am I allowed to remember your name?' he wondered with withering scorn. 'Or should I perhaps bring someone else?'

The thought of Draco draped over another woman made her feel physically sick. Her chin went up. 'You can do what the hell you like,' she said with an unconcerned shrug.

As he stalked down the corridor he stopped short when he suddenly realised she was treating him like a sex object...so why the hell was he getting so irate about it?

Considering the way they left off, Jane wasn't sure what sort of reception she would get from Draco at the cocktail party. She was not looking forward to making a solo entrance and was glad she bumped into Joe and Luciana in the cloakroom as she handed in her silk wrap.

'Oh, wow, you look gorgeous!' Luciana exclaimed. 'I just love that dress. I can't believe it's the same one you bought in that vintage shop.'

Jane nodded a little self-consciously. 'Thank you, it needed a few tweaks.' She had stripped the dress down to its basics, removing the fussy frills around the neckline and the gaudy sash to reveal the simplicity of the blue silk underneath, the bodice that hugged and the bias-cut skirt that flared and swished around her calves.

'The shoes are new though,' she said, extending a slim ankle for inspection. 'I haven't got a clue why I packed them,' she admitted, looking at the pointy-toed spiky heels that had been a bargain buy in a sale…impractical but beautiful. 'I felt tall until I saw you, Luciana.'

The willowy young Italian smiled. 'I thought Joe might take me out somewhere. That's why I put this in.' The Italian girl laughed and gave a twirl, the beaded hem of her mini rattling as she did so.

Her English boyfriend, a good foot shorter and wearing a tweed waistcoat over his best jeans, responded with a loud, *'Bella!'* in a Liverpudlian accent and dragged her in for a kiss.

Watching their youthful and carefree antics made Jane feel a hundred years old. They were so spontaneous, so unencumbered with complications—so in love!

'It's gorgeous. If I had your legs,' Jane said, admiring the girl's slim, endless legs with envy, 'I'd wear it every day. You make me feel like a dwarf.'

The laugh, a rather grating artificial sound, made them all turn.

'You aren't tall, are you?' The remark came from a stranger who was peeling off a fur wrap.

Her heels made Jane's look like flats and her silver dress, which appeared glued to her body, displayed every curve of her lush, voluptuous figure.

'Hello,' Jane said a little awkwardly, because the normally warm and welcoming Luciana had not responded at all beyond taking her boyfriend's arm in a tight warning grip.

The blonde with the hard eyes was looking Jane up and down. Her expression suggested she had awarded Jane a grudging five and a half, and Jane might have been amused except there was *something* about this woman.

Reproaching herself for judging by appearances, Jane forced a smile.

'So are you all part of this *green* thing?' the blonde asked with another artificial-sounding laugh.

Jane nodded.

'So you are staying in one of those awful rooms?' She made the en suite facilities sound like hovels and Jane, who had visited Luciana in hers, knew they were anything but.

Luciana, who was normally friendly to everyone, stood, her lips tight, but, making an obvious effort to be polite in the face of the other woman's rudeness, intervened.

'Joe and I are, but Jane is staying up in the palazzo, as a guest. She has her son with her.'

The woman's patronising smile faded and one of her pencilled brows rose as her spiteful, speculative stare turned towards Jane. Her interest was of the malicious variety, something in those heavily made-up eyes making Jane feel uneasy.

'In the palazzo, how very nice,' she trilled back, making it sound not nice at all. 'I am not allowed up there any longer.' She placed one heavily ringed hand on her heart and, adopting the persona of a heroine in a Victorian melodrama, revealed in a throbbing voice, 'But it was once my home.'

Jane heard Luciana mutter something in her native tongue under her breath. It did not sound complimentary.

Home…?

Even though the woman's facial muscles were no longer capable of moving, Jane sensed her frown as she turned her attention back to her.

'Have we met before?'

'I don't think so.'

'Oh, I think so, and I never forget a face…' The woman tapped the side of her head. 'It will come to me.'

It sounded like a threat.

'Do you know her?' Jane asked as the blonde made her sinuous way ahead of them, where a door swung open and she vanished, along with the sounds of chatter and laughter that had spilled out.

'*Sì*, I will explain later,' Luciana said in a confidential aside behind her hand as a pair of servers in smart black trousers and white shirts passed by carrying trays containing arrays of edible works of art, minuscule but pretty. 'Take no notice of her. She is an utter bitch and I have no idea why she is here tonight except if it is to cause trouble.'

Mystified by this uncharacteristic venom, Jane wondered who the woman was and what her connection was to the palazzo. She'd lived there?

Could she be an ex of Draco's…? It was as hard to imagine Draco being seduced by a predatory older woman as it was to imagine him moving one of his overnight girlfriends in.

Jane dismissed the possibility almost immediately. The woman's face might be lifeless, but her eyes were not young. She fell into step with the young couple as they stepped through the open door.

Jane blinked. The overnight transformation was dramatic! The double doors that interconnected the four meeting rooms had been opened and the space was impressive.

Music provided by a string quartet was playing at one end of the room and serving staff circulated with silver trays among the beautifully dressed guests. There were a few jeans and jumpers from the usual suspects, but even they looked less crumpled than usual as they mingled with the sprinkling of movie stars, politicians and aristocracy.

Jane found herself wondering where she fitted in, and then realised she probably didn't as she grabbed a glass as it was offered. A couple of sips made her feel a little less panicky.

'Jane…?'

Jane tried to place the tall, slim, good-looking young man in a blue velvet tux and then it hit her.

'Jamie?'

Draco's half-brother, no longer a skinny beanpole of a kid, grinned and hugged her. 'My God, what are you doing here?'

'I keep asking myself the same thing,' Jane admitted.

'So are you and Draco back together?'

Jane felt her heart clench. 'No, nothing like that. We are…not a couple.'

Never would be a couple, the depressing thought flashed into her head.

Never really had been a couple. When she had said yes to his proposal, she had not known him… Had she loved him? She had certainly been infatuated by him, but her feelings then, strong though they had been, were a shadow of what she felt now. What she felt now was deeper, stronger, and when she saw him with Mattie she knew what an incredible father he would be one day.

Had his feelings changed too?

She pushed away the question, aware that once she allowed herself to indulge in wishful thinking it would be all the harder to face the reality of the situation when it came time to say goodbye. She had to live in the moment and accept that the moment meant something very different to her than it did to Draco.

Her shaking hand slopped a bit of her wine, and just when she needed it, she thought, draining what was left in the glass.

'You all right?' Jamie asked, taking the glass from her fingers and putting it down on a side table.

'Fine. So Draco didn't mention I was here?'

'We've hardly had a chance to speak. You were the last person I expected to see after—'

CHAPTER TEN

Jamie's eyes widened and he winced. 'Sorry, I didn't mean it to sound like that.'

'It's all right. I know what you mean.'

'You haven't changed at all,' he marvelled.

'You have,' Jane said, taking a step back to look at him.

'I'm flattered you didn't recognise me,' he joked. 'And—'

'Jamie, my darling boy!'

Jane could almost feel the energy being sucked out of the young man. She could see the gawky boy he had once been as he froze, turning slowly towards the voice.

The connections were being made in her head as she watched the blonde from earlier kiss the air a foot or so either side of Jamie's face.

This was his mother, Draco's stepmother. Jane's heart went out to him.

'Oh, my darling, you still have the glasses, I see.' She shook her blonde head. 'They make you look so geeky. Tell him,' she said, appealing to Jane. 'Contact lenses or, better still, laser surgery and…' She brushed an invisible crumb off her son's immaculate lapel, her lips twisting into a grimace of distaste. 'You always were a messy little—' The eyes swivelled slyly towards Jane. 'Aren't you going to introduce me to your friend? I'm Jamie's mother. I know, before you say it, I look too young.'

Jane, who hadn't been about to say anything of the sort, took a deep breath. 'How lovely to meet you— again,' she said calmly, not even bothering to disguise her insincerity. 'So sorry, but Jamie promised me this dance.'

Jamie blinked at her as she inclined her head to the empty space in the centre of the floor, her eyes flashing a message.

'Nobody is dancing,' the woman pointed out petulantly.

Jane took Jamie's hand and laid it on her waist, and after the slightest pause he placed his other in the small of her back.

'They are now!' she cried as they twirled away.

'Thank you,' Jamie said quietly as he held her eyes, gratitude shining in his.

Jane could see the beads of sweat along his upper lip and her heart went out to him as she reflected how terrible it was that a mother-son relationship could be so toxic.

'Oh, hell, thank God you can dance!' she said a few moments later and was pleased to feel some of the young man's rigid tension relax as they moved to the music.

'A lot better than you,' Jamie retorted. 'You have trod on my feet three times.' He laughed and leaned in, his expression serious as he emphasised, 'Really, thank you for that.'

'Any time,' she said, meaning it. 'I suppose I've broken some rule by dancing,' she said, half gloomy, half laughing.

'What's the worst that can happen?' Jamie said.

Jane lowered her eyes and thought, It already has.

She'd been hiding behind the illusion that she was in charge, she set the rules and boundaries, which meant she was safe, but, for all the smoke and mirrors, it was self-delusion. She wasn't.

She was in love with Draco and the heartbreak coming her way was inevitable, but in the meantime, she told herself fiercely, she was going to enjoy every precious moment of it.

'Wow!' The dizzying circle of alternating despair and determination in her head was broken as she allowed herself to be manoeuvred around another couple to avoid a head-on collision.

The floor was now quite crowded. Several couples of varying abilities had joined them, and the quartet had reacted by switching seamlessly to a slow, dreamy waltz number.

'Wow, you are so good at this,' Jane said truthfully.

'When I didn't make the soccer team, Draco advised me to find something I was good at. Turned out that women like dancers more than they like jocks, or it might just be me,' he said smugly.

Jane laughed. 'Oh, you sound so like Draco.'

'I'm not sure I'd take that as a compliment, Jamie. Do you mind if I cut in?'

Grinning, Jamie released Jane and as Draco bent to say something in his ear he nodded, flashed a grin at

Jane and mouthed thank you before threading his way through the dancers.

'May I have this dance, *cara*?'

She nodded, feeling suddenly incredibly shy. 'I should warn you, I'm not a very good dancer.'

'I think that is for me to say.'

He did not pull her into his arms immediately. Instead he took her elbows and held her a little away from him, his head dipping as his glittered dark stare swept down her body.

Jane felt the quiver start deep inside until her entire body was engulfed by a hot tide of sexual awareness... It seemed crazy to her at that moment that she had ever convinced herself she could enjoy him and then walk away.

'You look very beautiful.'

It was not the words, it was his voice, his eyes, it was everything about him that stalled her brain. She knew they were surrounded by people and she ought to be acting normally—she had forgotten what normal was!

'I'm not a very good dancer,' she said as his hand came to the small of her back. She could feel the warmth of his splayed fingers through the silky fabric.

'You said that.'

'Did I?' she said vaguely. He took her hands, which lay loosely at her sides, her fists clenched white, and placed them on his shoulders and put his one hand on her back between her shoulder blades, the other to her waist.

'Follow me.'

A bubble of laughter emerged as a strangled choking sound through her clenched teeth as she realised she would probably follow him over a cliff.

No, you wouldn't, said the stern voice in her head. Because a) he wouldn't ask, b) you are a mother, so your first responsibility is to Mattie, and c) you wouldn't be standing on the edge of a cliff because you are scared of heights.

This sense-inducing line of logic at least gave back the ability to breathe, but only shallowly, as he began to move, no, they began to move as one unit. Draco didn't have Jamie's fancy steps, or if he did he wasn't using them, it was just silky smooth harmony and hypnotic sway, the closeness intense but, in a contradictory way, seductively soothing.

Jane's nostrils flared as she breathed in the warm male scent of him, revelling in the coiled strength of his hard body. Enclosed by his arms, she felt cut off from everything but him—he was everything.

His breath was on her hair and then her neck. 'I saw what you did.'

'I felt like dancing and your brother is a very good dancer.'

'Better than me…?'

'Much better.'

His chest lifted in a laugh. 'Really, *cara*, it was good of you to rescue him. She…his mother, Christina.' On his lips the name sounded like a curse. 'She is a vindictive bitch, utterly selfish, but, more than that, vicious, and let's just say that when they were handing out maternal instincts she was not at the back of the queue. She missed it totally.

'She traumatised him when he was a kid. Her voice could make him shake. It wasn't physical abuse, it was—' He heaved a deep sigh. 'The best thing she ever did for Jamie was desert him.'

'Why did you invite her?'

'Invite?' he exploded, looking outraged, then, in response to her widened eyes, lowered his tone as he explained. 'It seems like she came as a plus one and ditched her escort the moment the helicopter landed. I don't know why she's here but I'm assuming it's not concern for our mental well-being! Look, let's not talk about her just now...' he said, drawing her into his body.

Jane had no issue with this suggestion.

She lifted her head and placed a hand on his chest. 'Draco, the music has stopped.'

He stood still and Jane caught a dazed look drift across his face as he saw the people leaving the floor and others moving in to take their places as the music struck up a jazzy number. Well, as jazzy as a string quartet went.

Jane watched his previously distracted expression clear as he scanned the room with a practised eye. 'There are people I have to talk to.'

Was she imagining the underlying hint of frustration in his lean face? 'We will talk later,' he said, pulling back, but leaving his hand on the base of her spine as they left. The gesture felt possessive, and she found herself wondering if other people saw it that way.

'Maybe we should be careful. People might make the connection, put two and two together and—' She gestured with her head. A few loose curls had already escaped the Grecian coil at her neck that had taken ages for someone whose idea of a hairdo was a comb and shake. 'I think people are looking.'

He stopped as they reached the edge of the area that had become an impromptu dance floor and tugged her around to face him. 'Of course they are looking, you look… That is your second-hand dress?'

She felt his warm gaze move over her body. 'Vintage,' she corrected, her green eyes laughing up at him. 'It is also much greener to shop locally, as you should know,' she reproached, tongue in cheek.

'So true, and here is someone you might like to educate on that subject… Tabitha Greenwood, Jane Smith… Tabitha is a—'

'I know who Miss Greenwood is!' Jane protested, flushing as she smiled at the fashion designer with the international reputation, who was instantly recognisable even if she had changed her hair colour from jet black to platinum blonde. 'Hello,' she said to the woman studying her with open curiosity through a pair of massive pink designer glasses.

'Jane was just lecturing me on waste in fashion. She's a big fan of charity-shop bargains.'

'Actually, I am.' She slung a look up at Draco. 'He is putting words in my mouth and I am quite capable of speaking for myself.'

'Well, that is telling you!' cried the other woman, looking amused by the interchange.

'Actually my dress—'

'Vintage,' the designer cut in, casting an expert eye over the blue silk gown. 'It is gorgeous and, I suspect, updated a little?' She quirked a quizzical eye at Jane, who nodded.

'I can't really do frills.' She grinned and made an expressive sweeping gesture towards her foot. 'I'm too short.'

The other woman, who was a sturdily constructed five nine, smiled back. 'But perfectly formed, as they say, don't you think so, Draco?'

Draco gave her a sardonic smile and said nothing.

'See you later, enjoy...' He paused and swung back. 'Have you eaten anything more substantial than a canapé?'

Jane, who hadn't had a canapé yet and was very aware of the speculative gleam in the birdlike gaze of the designer, shook her head in irritation. 'Don't fuss.' To prove a point she grabbed a handful of canapés from a tray and put them one by one into her mouth. The last one was rather delicious. 'Happy now?' she challenged.

Never as happy as when I am looking at you.

The extraordinary recognition just popped fully formed into his head.

As there was no answering grin, her own smile faded. His expression was about as revealing as bulletproof steel shutters. It made her realise that she had not seen that closed-off look in a while, and she really hadn't missed it!

Watching the tall figure stride away, the two women exchanged glances.

'What was that about?' the older woman wondered.

'Not got a clue,' Jane said with a tight, strained smile. 'I'm here for research purposes and, of course, the champagne,' Tabitha added, grabbing a fresh glass from a passing waiter. 'These days you have to go green or go out of business. What about you?'

'I have a place on the course here.'

'Yes, but you already know Draco.'

'What makes you say that?'

The older woman threw back her head and laughed. 'It's pretty obvious, my dear. I hear you're staying in the palazzo? And yes,' she added in response to Jane's expression, 'I am a nosy old biddy, but I'm only saying what other people are thinking after that dance.'

Jane looked at her in dismay. 'I'm staying at the palazzo because I have my baby with me and Draco kindly put us up there because it's quieter.'

'A baby...?'

Jane could see the wheels turning and thought, Beam me up!

'Mattie, the baby's parents,' she said quietly, 'they died. I'm his guardian.' There was some relief in fessing up even if it was to the wrong person.

The mockery in the other woman's eyes faded, to be replaced by compassion that brought tears to Jane's eyes. 'Oh, my dear, how tragic.' She squeezed Jane's shoulder. 'I've never been a mum, it just didn't happen, but, you know, I think you will be a really good one. Come on, I have a friend who I know would love to meet you. She is very into vintage as well.'

As Draco did the handshakes and smiles he was aware of Jane in the middle of a diverse gaggle of people who seemed to be having more fun than anyone else in the room.

He felt a swell of admiration, a possessive pride that he knew he didn't deserve as he watched Jane shine, her natural warmth drawing people to her.

A phenomenon he understood totally.

It seemed bizarre that he'd been concerned she would not feel comfortable today. His concern had been misplaced. Four years ago it wouldn't have been. If he'd shown a shred of empathy back then, if he had actually picked up on the signs of stress…and had a conversation about it…the wedding might have gone ahead.

He felt a surge of self-disgust because he *had* picked up on the signs, but he had ignored them, filing them under inconvenience, because beautiful, desirable Jane would always be there, smiling at his elbow and fire in his bed.

It was more difficult to slip away than Jane had imagined but she finally managed.

'You running away from the ball?'

She was good at running, he reminded himself, nursing the old hurt, channelling old anger and resentment as a barrier when he felt himself getting closer to her, when he found himself thinking *family* when he played with Mattie.

Lately the embers of old hurt were harder to kick into life. Logic suggested that it was probably a good thing she would be leaving soon, but he found it hard to summon much enthusiasm because logic was a casualty of the passion that burnt between them, a passion that had not as yet burnt itself out.

* * *

Jane's breath caught at the sound of his deep voice. She ignored her thudding heart as she turned, channelling calm that was not even skin deep.

Being around Draco made her feel more alive somehow. His presence heightened her perceptions. A moment before she hadn't noticed the romantic twinkle of the thousands of white fairy lights that wound around the trees that lined the path back to the palazzo, or the scent of rosemary and pine in the soft sea breeze or the moon that put blue highlights in Draco's dark hair and accentuated the perfect angles and planes of his face.

His dark jacket hung open, the white of his shirt was dazzling, and underneath was the silky brown skin and the light dusting of body hair, the directional line that vanished as it met… She inhaled and thought, Pull yourself together woman—focus!

Not on that, she thought as her eyes sank just a little lower.

Cheeks hot, she dragged her eyes to his face. 'Well, I was not running.'

So no excuse for the breathless delivery.

She lifted her heavy silk hem, exposing her calves, and angled a wry grin at her feet, a really safe place to stare at. 'Not in these, and this was officially designated a party, not a ball, also no relation at all, as far as I know, of Cinders.'

'That is a very thorough analysis. I will always come to you for fact-checking. I will rephrase—walking away from the party.'

She tried to smile but it just wouldn't come. 'I want to head back to check on Mattie. Yes, I know Val can cope,' she added quickly, anticipating his response, 'but he's not been himself today.'

'Mother's instinct?' He watched her flinch and took a step closer, a concerned frown tugging his brows.

She shook her head. 'No, just observation,' she said, ignoring the slug of guilt and changing the subject. 'Tonight was a success for you. You must be pleased.'

Was he?

Draco hadn't even thought about it, and the success of this project should have been his main focus—tonight was part of that. Yet the entire evening he had felt as though he was playing a part, saying the right things, and occasionally the wrong thing, while all the time his eyes had been searching for a flaming redhead.

He had brought Jane here with some vague idea of making her hurt the way she had hurt him. At some point the plan had lost impetus and derailed itself...and ironically the only person hurting, it seemed to Draco, was him.

The pain had centred on his frustrated primal urge to possess her. Being lovers ought to have solved that issue, leaving him to walk away when the hunger had burnt itself out. The hunger was still raging and now it came with excess... He refused to call it emotional baggage, but what else could you call it when he looked at her, so small, so vulnerable, so bloody-minded and stubborn he kept feeling the alien urge to protect her.

It wasn't meant to be like this.

Sex should not be like this. It should be uncomplicated. It was one of the most uncomplicated things in
life, a need that he prided himself on being able to control. It never got in the way of the more important things.

'It was a success for you,' he countered finally.

'I had fun,' she said, a wistful note in her low voice.
Not with me!

'It will be something nice to remember when I go back
home,' she said with an upbeat smile. She'd die before
she'd let him know how much it hurt to say that. 'And I
have made some friends I will keep in touch with, and
young Val is showing me her brother's apiary tomorrow.
I have had a crash course in beekeeping and its importance, not just to the rural economy, but basically the
future of the world.' She painted on a smile.

'Yes, he is very entrepreneurial. He's got orders from
a major London store,' Draco, who wasn't at that moment interested in bees, told her. 'You could come back?'

The suggestion seemed to surprise him as much as
it had her.

'To see your friends, Luciana and her boyfriend—'

'Joe? Won't he be going home next week too?'

'He and Luciana have taken out a lease on one of the
studios in the creative hub.'

This was news to Jane. 'Jamie seemed shocked to
see me here.'

'I didn't think he was going to get away. He was playing a chess tournament, but it got cancelled.'

The tiredness that had been kept at bay by adrenaline
was hitting home as Jane took the few steps across to a

carved wood bench, situated to make the most of the incredible view out to sea, which was utterly spectacular. At night the ocean was just another shade of darkness in the distance and the light and magic came dappled from the fairy lights threaded through the branches.

'He's still in college though?' she said, trying to work out the age of the teenager.

'His last year at school. He's thinking of turning professional when he leaves.'

'Professional?'

'Chess. He is really very good.'

Jane searched his face curiously. 'Do you mind? Don't you have plans—?'

'I would prefer he went to university,' Draco admitted. 'But that's probably because I missed out. I want Jamie to have freedom, the opportunity to do what he wants and change his mind if that's what he needs.'

'Why did you miss out?'

'My father was not the most caring of parents.'

Jane thought about the scar on Draco's skull and realised that he had stayed around to make sure that Jamie didn't suffer the same way. 'His mother—?' She stopped and shook her head. 'Sorry, I don't mean to pry.'

'Christina used him like an accessory,' Draco responded, his voice as flinty and unforgiving as iron filings. 'And while he was a pretty cute baby she had him wheeled out by nanny for the photo ops and charity events, but Jamie had issues with his eyes. He needed corrective surgery and wore thick glasses…' His lips thinned with distaste. 'Not so cute, apparently,' he finished with contempt. 'She moved on from him and this place and our father had zero interest in him.'

Jane remembered how the comment about his glasses had paralysed Jamie, and her heart broke for him. 'Poor Jamie.' Or maybe lucky Jamie, because he'd had Draco around to protect him.

'Our father was a man in thrall, so weak so…she was like a drug for him. He had no pride, no sense of duty to this place.' He gestured towards the spotlit palazzo. 'He sold everything he could, sold off land, put families who had lived here for generations off the land, and I couldn't do a thing.'

Jane saw the echo of the remembered pain and frustration in his grim, almost haunted expression and her heart squeezed for the boy and young man he had once been.

'But now you can and you have,' she said gently.

Their eyes met and she watched the steel barriers sliding into place, until his face was an unreadable blank.

Frustration built up inside her. Just as he'd seemed to be opening up he had shut her out again.

'I should go back in, and get it over with,' Draco said, glancing back towards the lights of the building behind them. 'Christina isn't here for no reason.' It would be money. On the rare occasion she appeared it always had been, and if it wasn't for the fact she would stalk Jamie he would have sent her away empty-handed.

'And you are still protecting Jamie.'

'You like it here?'

Thrown by the abrupt change of subject and the tension in the atmosphere, she nodded. 'Obviously—what is not to like?' she said, her heart drumming.

'Does it actually need to end?'

Jane's thoughts raced as she closed her eyes against the chaos in her head… She took a deep breath and met his too intent dark eyes.

'What are you saying, Draco?' Not what you think, said the voice in her heart, except she didn't know what she thought. You couldn't kill hope.

Perhaps he saw something in her face because he said straight away, 'Obviously I am not proposing.'

The idea that he suspected her dreams was utterly humiliating.

'Obviously,' she said, enunciating each syllable with elaborate care while inside she felt like a total idiot.

'I think we both know, you before me possibly, that we would never have worked as a couple, but if we put our history aside there is no doubt that we have…something…?'

'Sex,' she intervened bluntly.

'Our personal relationship aside, your enthusiasm for this community, they would welcome you.'

'I know you look at me as the cure for some temporary testosterone imbalance!' she flung out wildly as she surged to her feet. 'But I don't see that as my life's work. I already have a life, and I don't want a temporary bit part in yours. My future doesn't involve you, Draco. Do you really think I would uproot Mattie, move to a different country where I have no friends…?' she exclaimed, breathless with indignation. 'My God, you have to be the most selfish, arrogant man in the universe!'

He ground his teeth. 'Why can't we discuss this situation like two sensible adults?'

'Because there is no situation and only one of us is a sensible adult. Thanks for the offer, Draco, but I'm already spoken for. My life is in England.'

The words thrown out conjured the image of Jane throwing open her cottage door, her bedroom door, to some faceless male figure. 'I'm here.'

'Your arrogance sometimes, Draco, is… You think you're the big selling point?' If that was what he thought it was hardly surprising, given that her feelings must have been obvious. 'I really need to go. I need to get back to Mattie.'

'You use him as an excuse. I'm not going to tell you what you want to hear to keep you here.'

The charge brought a hectic angry flush to her smooth cheeks. Presumably he thought she wanted to hear him say he loved her, and he was right, she realised, despising herself for holding onto a dream. 'I don't use anyone, Draco. I leave that to you! And you have no idea what I want to hear.'

She turned as the tears spilled, before he could see them overflow, before he could tell her that she had wanted to be used.

She had begged to be used.

Draco watched her stalk up the path, spine rigid, chin high. Even in the midst of his anger, justifiable anger, at her attitude, her delicious bottom under the silk, the sway of her hips were a major distraction.

As he watched she stumbled and fell off her spiky

heels and the instinct to go to her assistance made him surge forward, only to ask himself what the hell he was doing when she regained her balance and a string of curses drifted his way on the soft still night.

Without turning back, she bent down, pulled off her shoes and, with them dangling from the fingers of one hand, continued to walk up the incline.

The party was still in full swing and he had several people, donors and supporters, that he had to talk to.

He needed a few moments to compose himself before he could do his duty. Where was your devotion to duty a few minutes ago, Draco? he asked himself. He held himself to strict self-imposed rules, rules that meant he would never see his own father when he looked in the mirror.

Do you want rules or the woman you…? His clenched fist turned white as he fought the word before it formed in his head, words he didn't want to say, emotions he didn't want to feel.

He didn't need Jane. He didn't need any woman.

But he wanted her, how he wanted her.

'Going to follow her?'

CHAPTER ELEVEN

IT WAS THE voice that always elicited a visceral reaction of distaste that brought home the fact he had walked, not towards the building, but away from it and towards the palazzo.

'What are you doing here, Christina?' Despite the surgery, or maybe because of it, the years had not been kind to her, or maybe that was the sheer malevolence that he saw behind the perfect features, more perfect now than when she had married his father.

The blonde's over-pumped lips pouted. 'You forgot my invite.'

'The only invitation you'll get from me is to go to hell,' Draco informed her in a deceptively mild voice.

'Oh, well, if you're going to be like that...but I'll make allowances, Draco. Someone said no to you, so you are bound to be feeling a bit—'

'You were eavesdropping!'

'Before you ask, I heard enough.' The spiteful tinkle of laughter bounced off him. 'Poor Draco knocked back. You know, you reminded me of your father for a moment there.'

She watched the colour drain out of his face and

smiled a complacent cat-like smile that left her eyes hard as stone.

'Grovelling comes easy to the Andreas men.'

Denial was his first response.

Fury was his second and then—after he searched his memory for proof she was wrong—relief.

'Thank you,' he said softly.

He was not his father. He was his own kind of fool.

An expression of incomprehension flashed across the blonde's face.

'What for?' she said warily.

'For making me realise that I am nothing like my father.' His father had been many things, including deluded, but he had not been a coward, he thought in self-disgust. Whereas he had been a blind coward who had exiled himself from so many possibilities because he didn't have the guts to admit what he wanted.

To admit what he felt.

Jane hadn't walked away because he wasn't telling her what she wanted to hear, because he took pride in telling it the way it was…not sugar-coating it.

He had asked her to leave behind everything she knew and offered her nothing in return.

She had walked away because he was too much of a coward to say what she wanted to hear. He was too much of a coward to admit what he felt for her.

That he loved her.

He glanced at the spiteful face of the woman opposite, impatience, not anger, in his face now… He wanted this charade to be over. He saw his stepmother's expression falter a little, but she rallied and was back a moment later, her malicious smirk in place.

'She has quite a mouth on her, that girl. I wouldn't have thought she had it in her, but then you never can tell, can you? From those sweet and innocent butter-wouldn't-melt appearances.'

He did not move, and he did not raise his voice when he said softly, 'You will not speak of Jane. Is that understood?'

The older woman, shaken despite herself by the dark implacability in his eyes, took an involuntary step back.

Draco folded his arms across his chest. 'What do you want?'

'Oh, I'll get around to that, darling, but first tell your little playmate that I have remembered where I saw her... I never forget a face.'

'Leave Jane out of this. You will not go near her. I do not want to hear anything you have to say.'

'Oh, you will want to hear this. She has a baby, I hear—'

'Christina...' he said, a warning in his voice, a nerve clenching and unclenching in his lean cheek.

'Did I ever tell you about...? Well, probably not. But what was it—four years ago? I forget, but I had a little accident. I think Spiros was quite pleased to know he was still man enough, but thank God we were both on the same page.

'I went to a clinic in London. Mind you, if I'd known they had started taking NHS patients,' she said with a little moue of distaste, 'I would have gone elsewhere, but, still, it was sorted.'

The dismissiveness of how she said 'it' made him feel sick, especially when he thought about how for many women this was a decision that they did not make lightly, that they wept over. 'You had an abortion.'

'That's what I just said,' she replied with a bored sigh. 'I am a young woman, Draco.'

'Why would you think this would interest me?'

'Ah, yes, well, as I was being wheeled to the theatre I passed someone else on their way out...red hair, white face.'

His lean face froze, the skin pulled tight across his sharp cheekbones as her meaning hit home. 'Liar!'

'Ask her yourself if you don't believe me.'

'I won't, I don't need to,' he said, even though they both knew he would.

And when he did?

Having delivered her malice-laden bomb, his darling stepmother vanished, leaving just the stink of her choking perfume behind, where to and with whom he frankly didn't give a damn!

Draco didn't give her the satisfaction of knowing that her poisonous darts had found fertile ground. He pulled it together and went back into the party or—as his inner voice said—did a Draco Andreas.

Next thing he knew he'd be referring to himself in the third person.

It was a good two hours later when he finally left and made his way through the grounds to the palazzo.

Four years...four years...he tried not to connect the

dots but by the time he entered the hallway they were a solid directional line.

He remembered the small scars on her smooth belly and the way she had dismissed them, not quite meeting his eyes when he mentioned them. Could they be connected to…?

An image of her holding the baby floated into his head. She was the perfect mother to another man's child.

Had she aborted his child?

He prided himself on not being judgmental when it came to the choices women made about their own bodies, but this was not impersonal, this was as personal as it got—his child. Grief of something lost to him tightened like a fist in his belly. His hands clenched at his sides. This was not something he could consider with cool neutrality.

He had to know.

She owed him some sort of explanation.

Would she be waiting for him to climb into bed beside her? He pushed away the image that floated into his head of her warm and soft, sweet-smelling body as she smiled a sleepy smile and reached for him.

As he entered the nursery corridor he slowed slightly, a frown puckering his brow. His housekeeper, wearing a dressing gown, and a member of her team were standing there deep in conversation.

'Livia… What is happening?'

Their expressions and the tears on the normally cool and collected face of the housekeeper made his stomach muscles clench in anticipation. It didn't take a genius to see that he was not about to hear good news.

It wasn't good news and, though he had to prompt the woman, he eventually got the story.

Mattie was ill, a doctor had been called but they didn't know when he would be here, because some form filler on the other end of the line was asking so many questions before they would confirm his attendance.

Draco walked in, and took in the scene at a glance.

The baby was crying in his crib, young Val standing beside it, tears streaming down her face, while Jane, still wearing the blue silk dress, had the phone in her hand. White-faced, she looked haunted and was visibly shaking, but there was a firm determination in her voice as she spoke.

The anger that had kept up the walls of emotional isolation he had been sheltering behind dissolved. Everything inside him ached for her. He felt her fear and desperation.

'No, not that I am aware of. No, I am not the baby's biol—'

'Give it to me.'

'Draco!' she cried, relief in her voice as he took the phone from her limp grasp.

She took a step away, her arms wrapped protectively around herself, aware on one level that his presence could not make everything right but, oh, it was such a comfort just not to be alone.

He was speaking Italian but, unlike her, she could tell that he was in control of the conversation.

He was not begging, he was demanding, and it seemed to make all the difference. He paused occasionally, covering the receiver as he relayed a question to her in English before giving her response in Italian.

Finally he put the receiver down.

'Marco...' he began, pausing when she shook her head. 'He is the head of the paediatric intensive care unit. He will come with the air ambulance, which is already in the air, and in the meantime we are to cool Mattie down, open windows, strip off his sleep suit.'

'Thank you...oh, thank you! That is...just thank you, Draco,' she said, looking at him with shining eyes.

Draco nodded and walked across to the cot.

Trying to be as cool and calm as he appeared, Jane went to the crib. Mattie had stopped crying and the silence was somehow worse than that awful keening sound had been.

It was like undressing a rag doll and he was so hot.

'He is still very hot and so, so floppy.' Her voice broke as she turned away and laid her head against the warm solidity of Draco's chest, which was right there when she needed it.

She allowed herself the indulgence of staying that way for a few moments before she pulled herself together and stepped back.

'Val has gone to get a fan.'

At that moment the young woman arrived without a fan, but with welcome news. 'The helicopter is here. Oh, I am so, so sorry...'

'No, this is not your fault,' Jane said firmly as she clasped the younger woman's hand.

Draco watched her take the time even in the midst of her own fear to reassure the younger woman. A small snuffly cry made him glance down to the baby lying there, his sweaty face as pale as milk, and he felt things shift inside him. 'He looks—'

The door opened and a young man about Draco's age appeared.

Jane watched as they shook hands but did not waste time on pleasantries.

'Mrs—'

'Miss Smith, Jane,' she said.

'Well, let's have a look at this young man, shall we? While you tell me what happened.'

The examination was gentle but thorough.

'I suspect this was a febrile convulsion. We can confirm that when we have him at the hospital. For the present his temperature is high, and I will give him something for that before the transfer and also put a line in to give him some fluids.'

'Thank you,' Jane said, half scared to voice the question that was uppermost in her mind. 'Will he be all right?'

'I know it looks scary but little ones are very much more resilient than people think. I suspect there is an underlying infection.'

'You will run all the tests necessary.'

'*Sì*, Draco,' he said, turning to Jane. 'Try not to worry. He is in the best of hands.' His calm confidence worked its magic.

'Ah, here is Nurse now.'

A young man appeared, carrying a medical bag under each arm.

'We will get him ready for the transfer. You will be coming with us, I assume.'

Jane nodded as the two men bent over the cot, blocking her view of Mattie.

'Thank you,' she said in a quiet, sincere aside to Draco. 'You made that happen… I am so grateful. I will keep you in touch…'

'I am coming with you.'

'I should say, no, it's fine, but I'm not going to,' Jane admitted, feeling tears prick her eyes. 'I was so horrible to you.' She quivered, blinking away the salty tears of emotion trembling on the tips of her eyelashes.

'That is not important now.'

Her throat full and icy fear still gripping her belly, she nodded. 'I promised I would take care of him.'

Promised who? The dead father, he assumed. 'And you have, you are, you are an incredible mother.'

Her head bent, she sniffed, missing the look of pain that slid across his taut, lean features.

The helicopter journey was relatively short, the staff were really comforting, which Jane appreciated, and Draco's presence meant she didn't have to worry about following the conversations when they slid into Italian. The transfer into the hospital was performed with no issues and the medic's obvious competence was reassuring.

She had moved out of the way while the medical team gathered around Mattie, but she didn't take the seat offered. She couldn't sit still.

'He is in the very best hands,' Draco said, watching her.

She nodded. 'I know, it's just…'

The medical team moved away from the cot leaving one nurse at the bedside. The senior doctor walked across to them, smiling.

'Well, it is just as I thought, there is a viral infection, simple upper respiratory. He had a febrile convulsion, frightening, but not indicative of anything else. Now that his temperature is down and he is having his fluids replaced he will be back to normal very quickly. We will keep him in overnight for observation and, all being well, which I am sure it will be, he can go home tomorrow.'

Jane closed her eyes and gave a deep shuddering sigh before opening them and clasping the medic's hand in both of hers. 'Oh, thank you, thank you so much.' Before she released his hand with a self-conscious, 'Sorry.'

'Delivering good news is one of the best parts of my job.'

She watched Draco walk with him towards the door, her smile fading as she thought about the bad news he had to deliver too often, but not today and not to them.

'They will put a bed up in here if you wish to stay, though I have an apartment here where I will be staying.'

'No…no, I'll stay here, thank you.' She looked at him, noticing for the first time the lines of strain etched around his mouth. 'I am so sorry. I'm sure this is the last thing you wanted after—'

'Now is not the time.'

She set her lips in a straight line to stop the stupid quiver. He was allowed to sound brusque at the very least.

'You have my private number?'

'I don't have my phone.' She realised that she didn't actually have anything.

He seemed to read her mind. 'I'll organise some things for you and have them sent over.'

'It's half one in the morning, Draco.'

He looked at her with the hauteur and arrogance that often infuriated her and other times made her smile. At the moment it just made her feel safe.

'How is that relevant?'

'Silly me,' she said with a wobbly smile.

A small bag of essentials—toiletries, nightclothes and a change of underclothes—arrived an hour after he'd left, also a phone with a note attached saying, 'I've put my number in it' in Draco's bold, sloping hand.

Jane didn't anticipate getting any sleep, but, although the nurses were in and out all night to check on Mattie, she did manage two long stretches of rest, and after a wash and fresh clothes she felt almost human.

She was on her second cup of coffee when the doctor and Draco appeared.

Her eyes skated across Draco, noting the tension emanating from him, and the dark shadows under his incredible eyes, but then not everyone liked hospitals. Well, nobody liked hospitals, but for some people, often the sort of people who never had a day's illness in their lives, the medical environment, the reminder of human frailty, was tough to take.

'Good morning,' she said to the doctor, who returned the greeting before he walked across to the cot and consulted his tablet.

'Well, all the results are clear, no underlying issues. He is good to go.'

Jane bit her lip. 'He seems a bit cranky this morning?'

'He's got a cold so that's to be expected. You know the drill if his temperature goes up?'

She nodded. 'Are there any things he can't do?'

'Well, flying should be avoided for a little while. The upper respiratory infection would put a lot of painful pressure on his little eardrums, and it is hard to tell a baby how to release the pressure.' He turned to Draco. 'How are you thinking of getting back to the palazzo?'

'Would he be better staying in town for a day or so?'

'That would be the ideal solution for this young man.'

'Couldn't I drive?'

'It would be preferable to flying,' the doctor agreed. 'But the drive is… What, Draco?'

'Not an option,' Draco said flatly.

Jane clamped her lips over a retort that would no doubt have sounded churlish and ungrateful. She'd been happy for him to step in and smooth the way in an emergency situation, but now that had passed she really didn't want him to think he could carry on.

At some point she would have to make that clear.

'I could book into a hotel?'

Draco slid her an impatient look. 'Do not be ridiculous. You will be quite comfortable in the apartment. You will drop in and see the patient, Marco.'

'I will.'

Jane was pretty sure that doctors in his position did not do house calls, but she wasn't going to object.

'I don't want to be a nuisance.'

'Then stop talking rubbish,' Draco advised tersely.

She had the impression that had the doctor not been there he would have said more.

It was the doctor's presence that similarly stopped her protesting beyond an 'I'm not the sick one' when someone brought a wheelchair for her to sit in while she carried Mattie.

The surgeon wheeled the chair himself, which drew a few startled looks as they made their way to the main foyer of the ultra-modern building.

'Am I allowed to walk now?'

Draco, after a pause, moved to take Mattie from her arms.

Being held by Draco, the baby looked so tiny and the big-man-small-baby image, especially when the man was Draco, made Jane's throat tighten with emotion. But then, after the last twenty-four hours all her emotions were incredibly close to the surface, and her control, even given the traumatic events, seemed extremely fragile. Scratch the surface and she might start crying or laughing or shouting—most of the time she didn't know which direction her emotions would take her!

Free of the baby, she was able to get to her feet and shake hands with the doctor, who responded with a smile and added, 'Oh, I got the notes through from your family doctor and there was nothing significant in the medical history to be of any concern now or in the future.'

Jane nodded, relieved.

She had felt a moment of panic the previous night when asked if there was any medical history in the family he should be aware of. She had been forced to explain that she was not Mattie's biological mother. She had passed on Grace's name, pretty sure that, as their family doctor, the GP, who was also Mattie's godmother, would know the medical history.

'I should know about these things. It just didn't occur to me...' she admitted with a flash of lip-biting self-reproach.

The handsome medic shook his head and placed a comforting hand on her arm. 'Parenting is a balancing act. The most important thing is to enjoy the experi-ence—they grow up very quickly. You're doing a great job,' he added warmly before he left them.

Jane flushed with pleasure at the compliment.

Standing too far away to hear what was being said, Draco could see the warmth of the exchange and the pretty flush that brightened her heart-shaped face.

Jane secured Mattie in the car seat fixed in the not-child-friendly back of the low-slung powerful car that she suspected had never seen such a piece of equipment before. Now, if you were talking a fur stole or an item of feminine underwear...?'

Torturing herself with the visions that came with those items, she belted herself in beside him, her smile widening as he gave a gummy grin.

'Sit up front. There's no room back there.'

'There is for me,' she said stubbornly. Her knees pressing into the driver's seat was infinitely preferable to sitting beside Draco.

'What was that about?' Draco asked, looking at her in the rear-view mirror.

She looked bewildered.

'Marco is married with children.'

Jane blinked. 'You think I was flirting with Mattie's doctor!' The ludicrousness of the suggestion drew a gurgle of laughter from her, and beside her the baby joined in.

In no position to see the flash of shock in his eyes, all Jane heard was the silence from the front that was interrupted by the sound of a car horn.

Draco growled out something that sounded not polite in his native tongue and pulled out of the parking space. The memory of his claim that he was never jealous came back to mock him as he drove out onto the highway.

The hospital appeared to be situated on the outskirts of the city but every now and then Jane caught a glimpse of the spires and golden buildings of Florence.

It was beautiful but, strangely, she felt a sudden longing for home and all things familiar, and with the longing came an image, not of her cottage, but the palazzo, backlit by the warm afternoon sun.

The instinct shocked her. It could not be a good thing to become so attached to a place over such a relatively short period of time. Or maybe not the place, but the people—the person who lived there.

Well, you'd better become unattached very quickly, she told herself sternly as she stared at the back of Draco's neck, where even though he kept his dark hair short, it was beginning to curl.

She was quite glad there was zero conversation during the journey to Draco's apartment. Jane had been trying to name the different landmarks she glimpsed and wishing she had a guide book when tall wrought-iron gates ahead of them opened and he drove into a courtyard. The sound of traffic was muffled by the trees and the rows of fountains and lush greenery bordering the cobbled area.

'This is beautiful!' she said, craning her neck to see the wrought-iron balconies on the top floor of the three-storey building.

'Just the one apartment. We have offices on the ground floor, so no commute when I am here.'

'Offices?' she exclaimed, thinking, Not as we know it. 'Where are the cars?'

'It's a public holiday here this weekend and the main entrance to the office is around the other side of the building. There are not so many staff. It's just a small hub specialising in...' He paused and spared her the techno speak before adding simply, 'Mostly it is IT-based here, and my office. The pool and gym in the basement are open to the staff, but feel free.'

'I really don't think I'll have the time.' Or the inclination. She took a deep breath. 'I doubt I will be here long enough. As soon as Mattie is able, we will—' Then, because he might think that she was including him in the 'we', she added quickly, 'Me and Mattie?' Hearing the question mark in her voice, she flushed and, seeing his perceptive appraisal, wished the words unsaid.

It wasn't that she would ever give his proposal of staying serious consideration, which was just as well because, from his expression, he wasn't going to make the offer again.

Probably thinking he'd had a lucky escape. Last night

must have brought home that she and Mattie were a package deal and, as great as he was with Mattie, the baby was not his responsibility.

One day he'd have his own children.

'Me and Mattie. I think we might go directly home from here. I'll have already missed some of the course and it seems pointless—'

His strong jaw quivered as his dark glance slid from the baby to her. 'We will discuss things later.' The situation had necessitated a delay in confronting Jane, but there had been no lessening of his need to demand answers. He had spent a sleepless night with his stepmother's spiteful words pounding inside his skull like a jackhammer.

The careful placement of his words, the undercurrent in his voice, brought her head around to face him. She blinked, confused by the explosive tension pouring off him in waves, and turned back to the task in hand.

'Let me do that,' he interrupted, watching her struggle with the anchoring straps on the unfamiliar baby chair. Mattie, who had dozed off, carried on sleeping.

Jane eased herself out, taking care not to hit her head in the car built for looks and speed rather than its family-friendly qualities.

Draco did not hit his head and the car seat came away in two deft clicks and snaps.

Walking into the building's spacious entrance hall, he ignored a wide marble staircase and led her straight to a lift that whooshed upwards.

Inside the apartment was the same mix of ancient

and modern, eclectic contemporary pieces set against old stone and wooden panelling.

'I thought you'd like Mattie to sleep with you tonight.'

Jane wanted to ask if he would be sharing her room, but she didn't. The tension she had sensed earlier was even stronger in him now.

Draco couldn't wait any longer. 'I know.'

She blinked, met his hard dark eyes that glimmered like obsidian pools and it hit. He had overheard her conversation with Marco when she had told the doctor that she couldn't have children.

'Oh, I know I should have told you but I knew how you'd react.'

He just couldn't believe what he was hearing. 'So you knew how I'd react.'

'I suppose that some men might not mind, but I knew how badly you wanted a family, Draco, and at the wedding I knew I just couldn't do that to you.'

As a shaft of anger pierced him like a blade the faint white line around his sensually sculpted lips grew more defined. The idea that she had been carrying his child and known it, concealed it from him… It was almost as if he were standing outside his outrage. To embrace it would mean a loss of control, acknowledging a pain that he might never move beyond.

CHAPTER TWELVE

'YOU KNEW YOU were pregnant at the wedding.' It sounded so calm, so civilised, so careful. It was only careful to preserve the illusion that what he was feeling could be considered logically.

She felt utter confusion when he raked her with a cold stare.

'P-pregnant?' she stuttered out. 'What are you talking about…?' She suddenly realised to her horror that they were talking at cross purposes. 'No, that's not right…' She lifted her hands in silent appeal but saw her words had no effect on him. 'That wasn't how it was, Draco, just calm down and listen to me. I can explain.' Explain that she had wanted to guard her secret. She'd fooled herself that it had been to protect him but wasn't his anger justified? She had been protecting herself, like a wounded animal seeking a quiet corner to lick her wounds.

'It is a bit too late to lie now. My stepmother was at the same abortion clinic as you. She remembers you well. So don't try and deny it!'

Never forget a face.

The woman's comment came back to Jane.

Like cracking a safe, the clicks in her head continued until the truth of what he was thinking, of what he thought of her, was revealed.

The irony of what he imagined the truth to be was not lost on her as her horrified despair became fury at the flick of a switch.

'I'm not going to try and deny it,' she told him, all cold disdain and hot flashing eyes.

'So you admit it?' he condemned, past the point of taking prisoners. For the past twenty-four hours he had imagined she would deny it and they would laugh together, because how could the woman he knew was willing to sacrifice everything for her child be capable of that? But no, that wasn't happening. This was the reality that he had to accept.

'You know something? I think you want to think the worst of me.'

'Do not try and deflect.'

'Yes, I was at that clinic. I was an emergency admission.'

His anger faltered for a split second, but then he remembered her saying that she had known at the wedding and she had hidden the truth from him.

'You had a miscarriage?' Alone, hurting, afraid. He took a deep breath. 'Talk to me. I will listen.'

It was the fact he thought he was being the big man that really got to her. 'Oh, wow, that is so good of you,' she drawled, her voice dripping with sarcasm.

'I just want to know why,' he blasted out, finding her anger and aggression bizarre. 'Do you not think I am owed that much? It was my child.'

'No, Draco, it wasn't your child. There was no child,' she told him bleakly. 'I did not have a miscarriage. I couldn't have a miscarriage because I can't have a child.'

'You are talking...?'

'I saw a doctor two days before our wedding. He told me that I had severe endometriosis. Look it up,' she added in response to his blank look. 'It was,' she admitted with a slightly hysterical laugh, 'a relief. I had a name for the debilitating pain and the symptoms. The relief didn't last,' she added, turning her haunted green eyes to his face. 'Then he delivered the double triple-whammy—that I would never likely be able to have children.'

'But you have Mattie.'

Her glimmering smile now held sadness. 'I do, I have Mattie,' she said, her chin lifting. 'But only because his parents died. You remember Carrie? Mattie is her son.'

'Why on earth didn't you say so right at the beginning? You let me think...'

'Everyone in the village knows. I suppose I just assumed that you'd find out and it was quite nice to pretend...no!' she self-corrected with a fierce little shake of her head. 'Mattie is my son.'

He had wanted answers and he was getting them but not the ones he had anticipated. 'What were you doing in that clinic, then?' he growled, finding it disorientating to have things no longer slotting into place in his head.

'I was there because my endometriosis had caused internal issues, bleeding.' She couldn't bring herself to say life-threatening but the situation had been. 'And I needed emergency intervention.'

'Surgery…? The scars…?'

She nodded. 'From the laparoscopy.' She cleared her throat and struggled to organise her thoughts when all she wanted to do was wail. 'I was spared a major incision.'

She spoke so quietly, without any emphasis, but her words cut into him as brutally as the suggestion—a knife-blade.

'The operation was a success, they tell me.' She was aware she should have felt more grateful than she had at the time. 'And I have to say it changed my life, the pain, not just monthly…but I know you are not interested.'

There was no condemnation, just a bleak acceptance in her words that made guilt rush into his head.

'Your stepmother is a bitch, and I am only quoting,' she concluded with a bitter laugh. 'But when this person you so despise—no, loathe—when she spilled her poison you were very happy to believe her.

'You know something, Draco, I think you wanted to see the worst in me, and yes, I know I should have been brave enough to tell you before the wedding, but I was in denial.' She pushed her fingers through her curls and they spilled out like fire against her pale face. 'And, you see, I always knew that you wanted a family more than you wanted me. I was just meant to be… What do they call it? The silent partner, and I loved you so very much that it didn't matter.

'But I am not that person any longer and it does matter. It matters that you believe I am…' As her voice became blurred by tears that she desperately blinked away, she shook her head. 'I would have been happy to be the silent partner but not now. The least I would expect of a partner or even a lover is that they believe in me.

'I apologise for not telling you the truth for that terrible wedding debacle. I should have been braver, but it is hard to know you can't give the man you love the only thing he wants.'

'Don't, Jane!' Draco breathed, holding up his hands as if to physically fend off her words.

'What? Don't tell you that I loved you? That I wanted to give you what you wanted more than anything?'

She saw his twisted tortured expression and said with a bitter laugh, 'Oh, I know that you didn't love me, even then I knew that and I… I felt inadequate… I felt…' She swiped a hand across her face and sniffed, adopting a tough expression that she was a million miles from feeling. 'Less than a woman.'

Jane was so caught up in her emotions that she barely registered the stricken expression on his face.

'I loved you and I wanted…' She inhaled, her chest lifting. 'But I believe, I know, that I deserve more than you are able, or willing, to give me. But all that is irrelevant. I can't give you babies, Draco, no beautiful babies, no heirs. So let's just say goodnight because this is getting so very, very tiring.'

With perfect timing the baby's bereft cries filled the room.

Jane looked at Draco one more time, drinking in the fabulous features, the man that she loved and always would, and turned away. The heart couldn't always have what it wanted. Sometimes reality got in the way.

It took her a good half an hour to settle Mattie and when she returned to the book-lined living area she knew without calling out that she was alone.

CHAPTER THIRTEEN

'So it is all right for us to travel.'

Marco, who had dropped in every day since they had been discharged, nodded his confirmation. 'If you think that is a good idea?'

'Is that a medical opinion?' Maybe he had read things into Draco's absence or maybe Draco had discussed the situation with him. What had he called it? she wondered bitterly. Awkward?

'No, not at all, it is a friend's opinion. And as a friend I say that you should not be carrying this news alone. You should tell him.'

'Tell who?' she said, feigning ignorance.

He raised a brow and said quietly, 'I was at the wedding.'

'Oh!' She swallowed. 'I didn't know, but I need to be where I don't feel so isolated.' She looked around the luxurious space they had stayed in for the last week.

It would have been easier if it had been an anonymous hotel but everywhere she came across signs of Draco's occupation: the book he'd been reading with its page marked, a scribbled note on a desk in his bold handwriting, the elusive scent of the male fragrance he used, the rows of freshly laundered shirts hanging in a wardrobe, which she had quickly slammed shut.

She couldn't stay here. She couldn't go back to the palazzo. The only option was to go home.

'I really need to think. I need to get my own head around it. I will tell him before I go,' she promised, her hands crossed across her chest. 'God, I can hardly believe it myself. Is it real?'

'It is real and you will do brilliantly. There is no medical reason your pregnancy will not go smoothly. And now I am speaking as a doctor.'

Draco's PR people were deliriously happy about an article written in a major financial journal praising his role in translating knowledge into strategies for driving forward a business model for a green revolution that had been picked up by multiple media outlets across the globe.

They had been confused by his lack of enthusiasm, but they did not recognise the irony. Draco was not deliriously happy. He was not happy at all.

Draco's two days of self-exile had made him realise that he was the architect of his own misery. He'd guarded his heart since childhood, not because it was smart or clever and definitely not wise, but because he was a coward!

People spoke of him as the man who had everything—he was living the dream. But he had been too much of a coward to even admit he had a dream.

A woman who was beautiful and smart had wanted to be with him and she had run away because she thought his only use for her was as a baby incubator. The shame he felt was intense.

It had taken more guts for her to run away than any he had ever shown. Jane had so much love to give and he had thrown it back in her face.

Jane hadn't run away. He was the one who had been running away all his life from feelings he was afraid to own.

Without Jane he had nothing.

Would she listen to him? He had no idea but he would try and he would never stop trying.

Later that morning, after Marco had left, Jane went online to book a flight. She had just completed the booking and was trying to work up the courage to call Draco when she heard a noise.

It made her pause because since her arrival she had barely registered that she was not alone in the building, if you discounted the formal person who appeared every day asking her to state her requirements.

In a brief moment of whimsy she had thought about requesting hair that didn't have a will of its own or the ability to not say the wrong thing at the wrong time... or maybe that was the right thing.

Though in the end she had been gifted her greatest wish.

The truth had still not bedded in her mind. She woke in the morning and then remembered. Despite the signs, if one of Marco's daily visits to check in on Mattie had not coincided with one of her really bad, 'can't pretend it's not happening' nausea events—not pretty—she still wouldn't have suspected.

When Marco had suggested that she might like to do a pregnancy test it had made her laugh—it beat crying. After she had reminded him of her medical history, to her amazement he had still thought it a good idea and produced one from his medical bag.

Jane was still reeling between joy and disbelief, but she had not changed her travel plans. Leaving was the only option open to her. While she felt guilty for not telling Draco the truth of Mattie's parentage, that guilt was outweighed by the hurt she felt that Draco had believed that she had had an abortion.

As she sat down to call him to tell him what he had a right to know, that he was going to be a father, she still had no idea what she would say. This time, though, she planned to be open and upfront. There had already been too many secrets.

Draco had always believed he knew what and who he was.

As he walked into the room that inner certainty had vanished. The truth was his confidence had never come from knowing who he was. It had always been about proving to the world and himself who he wasn't.

His father! His weak, selfish, pathetic father, and he'd become that man because of a toxic love.

The equation was simple: avoid love. See it coming and cross the street. He'd never needed to cross the street and then Jane had appeared.

His confidence had come from the conviction that he

couldn't be in love with anyone. Love was selfish and destructive, an indulgence for people who believed in fairy tales past childhood. He had made the argument until he was word perfect, using cold, hard logic and reason.

Now that conviction had been proved a lie. He loved Jane. The foundations he'd built his life on had crumbled and, instead of feeling lost and adrift, he felt liberated.

'Can I come in?'

'You are already in,' Jane pointed out, getting to her feet and walking away from her open laptop. 'And I'm the guest.' Had she overstayed her welcome? Was that why he was here? 'I was just about to ring you, Draco.'

'And now I am here.'

'I have booked our flights home, but first I wanted to apologise.' She swallowed and took a deep breath. 'Apologise for deceiving you. I should not have left you standing at the altar. I just wasn't brave enough to tell you why I had to. I took the easy route and ran.' She huffed out a sigh and squeezed her eyes closed. 'So many lies. I let you think I was Mattie's mother.'

Draco's eyes followed the direction of her glance to the baby.

'You are his mother in every way that counts. Is Mattie fit to travel?'

She gestured to the baby, who was lying on a vivid play mat, a toy stuffed in his mouth as he happily kicked. 'As you see.'

'Has Marco been calling in?'

'Every day. I'm assuming you asked him to?' Distancing himself. As far as she was concerned there was no other way to interpret the situation.

Draco nodded and dragged a hand through his dark hair. 'He won't tell me anything?' he ground out, his voice cracking with frustration. 'Just tells me he can't disclose medical details and if I want to know I should ask for myself.'

'And you came. That was good of you, but, as you see, Mattie is fine.'

'I expect you will tell me to go to hell, but actually I think I am already there! I know I let you down,' he said heavily. 'Believing the lies of that poisonous woman was unforgivable!'

'I was hurt,' she admitted with a catch in her voice. 'And hearing you say that means a lot to me.' Maybe more than you can ever know, she thought. 'But, Draco... there is something I need to tell you. Something that changes everything, but nothing,' she added bleakly.

Draco would never love her.

He took an impetuous step forward and as the light shone on his face Jane was shocked to see how drawn he looked as he caught her hands in his.

'No, let me speak. Ask you if you...' He released her and grabbed his head in both hands. 'Oh, Jane, I have been such a fool!' he cried out in an anguished voice she barely recognised. 'I love you. I have been the world's worst fool, a coward,' he bit out, his voice aching with self-contempt.

Nailed to the spot with shock, she just stared at him. Was this a dream?

'Please, Jane, tell me it is not too late... We have

Mattie. We don't need a baby.' He stepped forward and took her hands, lacing his long fingers in hers and bringing them up to his lips. 'All I need is you. All I ever needed was you, but I was afraid to admit my dreams, that you were my secret dream made warm, beautiful, brave flesh.

'This is no excuse, but I saw my father destroyed by a woman, but being without you—*my* woman—would destroy me. I am not a full person without you. Can you ever forgive me? Will you marry me? And this time it will be different because I am different. I am not afraid to tell you that I love you.'

Tears pricked her eyes as she read the anguish on his face, the blaze of hope and fear in his eyes.

She looked up at him, her heart shining in her face. 'I love you, Draco,' she said simply as she stepped into him, laying her heart against his heart and feeling his arms close tight around her.

'Not too tight...'

His arms dropped away and he looked at her anxiously. 'I hurt you?' He looked horrified at the thought.

'I just feel a bit queasy, that's all. Normally I love the smell of your soap but...'

'You are ill.' He went white. 'I will call...'

She shook her head. The rush of emotion too strong now to hold back the tears of joy that spilled out. 'It's fine. You see, I'm not ill. I'm having our baby, our miracle.'

Mattie, ignored for too long, let out a loud gurgle.

'A brother or a sister for you, little one, a playmate.' Draco placed a warm, protective hand on her flat stomach. 'It is safe for you? If not...' He shook his head. 'I will love our child, but I will never ever put you at risk, Jane,' he said sombrely. 'I hope you realise that.'

She slid a loving hand down his face, her vision misting at the sincerity in his voice. 'Marco says there is no danger, though it's possible I might need a caesarean.'

She had started crying and her heart was too full to tell him they were tears of joy.

'Do not cry, do not be afraid—you are not alone,' Draco soothed, cradling her face and kissing her lips with a blend of tenderness and passion that produced more tears.

'I'm not afraid. I'm happy I'll never be alone again,' she sobbed, her voice choked with raw emotion.

'If you don't stop crying I will have to kiss you.'

Jane smiled and let the tears flow, thinking, Bring it on!

* * * * *

If you just couldn't get enough of
His Wedding Day Revenge
*then be sure to check out these other dramatic stories
by Kim Lawrence!*

Innocent in the Sicilian's Palazzo
Claimed by Her Greek Boss
The Prince's Forbidden Cinderella
Her Forbidden Awakening in Greece
Awakened in Her Enemy's Palazzo

Available now!

HARLEQUIN
Reader Service

Enjoyed your book?

Try the perfect subscription for Romance readers and get more great books like this delivered right to your door.

See why over 10+ million readers have tried Harlequin Reader Service.

Start with a Free Welcome Collection with free books and a gift—valued over $20.

Choose any series in print or ebook. See website for details and order today:

TryReaderService.com/subscriptions